THE HIPPO GIRL AND OTHER STORIES

SHAH TAZRIAN ASHRAFI

hachette
INDIA

First published in 2024 by Hachette India
(Registered name: Hachette Book Publishing India Pvt. Ltd)
An Hachette UK company
www.hachetteindia.com

1

ISBN 978-93-5731-384-1

For sale in the Indian Subcontinent only.

Hachette Book Publishing India Pvt. Ltd
4th & 5th Floors, Corporate Centre
Plot No. 94, Sector 44, Gurugram – 122003, India

Typeset in Linden Hill 12/4.4
by Manmohan Kumar, Delhi

Printed and bound in India
by Manipal Technologies Limited

MIX
Paper from responsible sources
FSC™ C043100

Contents

To my Ammu and Baba
To my best friend, Imrul Kabir Emu
To the resilient people of Bangladesh

Brother

Hakim, Anwar, Rana, and I are running through the mango orchard. Yes, we are sick of crossing these same rows of trees and walking these same patches of grass but what else can we do? It's just another day in Kamalpara, so the blazing afternoon sun is no surprise. Hamza is chasing us. We enjoy it the most when he is the police and we're thieves. He has the speed to outrun a leopard and that thrills us. Before, before we arrived at Kamalpara, I mean, we had our entire village – Rahmatpur – to ourselves. We could run across the paddy and maize fields stretching and stretching to the horizon and kissing the clouds, across the forests skirting the riverbanks, past the mosque, the school, the madrasa, the post office, the rich landowners' moss-strewn bungalows, past whatnot. But in Kamalpara, we have only the mango orchard, the undergrowth behind the pit latrines and the pond, and the maze of black, grey, and white tents that has sprung up on the empty field opposite the school compound. Why? Because this village is not spacious enough to accommodate all of us and so the landowners' alliance sketched up the plan.

Here, we have to:

1. Wait in long lines to eat. Eat what? Bland rice and watery lentils. That too, twice a day! It would have been nice to

eat rice with meat and fish and vegetables three times a day like back home. This is why our ribs are always showing. Our veins, our eyes have begun to protrude. Stuffing such garbage down my throat, I cannot help but think that Satan himself has defecated inside the cooking pots.

2. Wait in long lines to bathe in the crowded green pond. I have lost count of the number of times I pushed a man or a boy out of my way so hard that they fell on the slimy green earth. My impatience always leads to verbal and physical altercations between them and the others they mistake for the perpetrator. It is a good thing that the spectacle serves as a nice timepass for the poor, stinking, sweating souls who cannot wait to jump in the water.
3. Wait in long lines to wash our clothes in the same pond. Spectacles abound here, too. Yesterday, I saw Sheela Chachi, a woman in her late fifties, getting repeatedly slapped by her daughter-in-law for stepping on her petticoat and tearing it near the ankle. Back in Rahmatpur, it was the other way around: Sheela Chachi used to beat her daughter-in-law for reasons we never knew; we only watched open-mouthed as she cried and moaned, and the broomstick rammed against her shins. When the military shot dead Sheela Chachi's son, she became entirely dependent on her daughter-in-law. Divine justice.
4. Wait in long lines to relieve ourselves in the latrines with broken roofs. This has to be the most frustrating part of my everyday life. Those waiting outside won't let you take a leak or a dump in peace. They keep banging on the flimsy tin door (which I worry will crack at the slightest touch one day) if you are in more than five minutes. In those moments, I want to snatch a gun from one of the patrolling fighters and shoot them dead.

5. Wait in long lines to fetch water from the rusty water tap. I like to observe squirrels squabbling among themselves as my empty plastic bucket grazes my legs. I also like to think of Shafi (I will tell you about him soon) because it is quiet with the unforgiving sun sucking up all the people's energy and rage like a passionate smoker.

On top of it all, we do not have our bicycles, marbles and ludo boards. So, my friends and I are stuck with playing tag, hide-and-seek, and manoeuvring discarded rickshaw tyres with long twigs and branches to see who comes first. At this point, I feel like I know the pathways zigzagging through the tents better than I know Rahmatpur. It is scary to think of it.

Now one might ask why we left our Rahmatpur to begin with. Ask a Pakistani soldier, and he will tell you why. We are Indian spies, he will say, lighting up his cigarette and glaring at you. We are Indian spies because we hide freedom fighters in our backyard. We are Indian spies because we want a separate country and do not want to taste their bayonets and bullets every single day. I hope one day their guns turn crooked like their heads. Our Indian spy-ness has made them set fire to our houses in Rahmatpur, shoot around like they were careless children pissing all over the washroom for fun, abduct men and women, and bring out tomatoes and eggplants from their faces and limbs, and of course, violate the women inside the camps they set up on our school campus. We ran with sacks tied around our torsos, with our cows and goats, as the gunfire roared behind us and thick plumes of smoke enveloped the coconut and palm trees.

What you need to know most importantly about Kamalpara is that it is a haven. Our freedom fighters, armed to the teeth with weapons they received from loyalists in the Pakistani army and snatched from dead Pakistani soldiers' shoulders, patrol the village perimeters day and night. Although they have not been able to penetrate the military presence in Rahmatpur, they regularly – once every week, at least – bomb other Pakistani outposts outside Kamalpara. They plant landmines on the roads snaking through the sal forests and bam! Onetwothreefourfivesix olive jeeps get blown to pieces. They hide in the bushes and rain bullets on the Pakistani jeeps and trucks. We hope one day they will kill every single soldier in Rahmatpur so we can go back and find our missing friends and bury our neighbours and play hide-and-seek and unwind with ludo and marbles inside the one-hundred-fifty-year-old ghostly Neelkuthi.

Despite all the gloom and doom, I count myself lucky. Alhamdulillah. I have my uncle – Mama, as we call him – with me. Unlike Anwar and Rana, whose t-shirts remain soaked with tears because the bullets raced through their parents' heads, I do not have to grieve and worry about my parents because Baba died before my twin (Shafi) and I slid out of our mother's womb and Ammu died right after we were done sliding out. Ever since, Mama has been taking care of me and Shafi as though he is our Baba and Ammu. Poor man is only thirty, stuck with us fifteen-year-olds. He was about to get married after inquiring with the imams about a potential wife who was as religious as he was – and if more religious, then amazing. But the Pakistanis had other plans, and the war trampled with its mud-stricken boots on his long-sought-after dream.

As for Shafi, I am a little worried about him. Because he is not here sweating under the raging sun and marking the days since we left Rahmatpur on the bark of a rain tree. Because he went to study at a renowned madrasa in Dhaka before the war began, owing to a generous scholarship our Islamic Studies teacher at the school had arranged for him on account of his goosebump-inducing talent – he recites the Qur'an as though it is a never-ending song leaking from his heart.

Our eyes are the same type of oval, our irises the same shade of green. Our noses are slightly crooked at the base. Our jawlines are free of chubbiness. Our voices are moderate – not too shrill, not too quiet. Our necks are slender, although he has a birthmark over his Adam's Apple. Distinguishing Shafi and me would have been hard if he did not have the habit of wearing thobe and kameez with a white skullcap all the time unlike normal kids who wore t-shirts and trousers.

He always scored the highest in the final exams while I was one of the last ten. He diligently helped Mama with the cleaning and cooking and grocery shopping. He even stood in for him and travelled to nearby villages to deliver baskets of cabbage and cauliflower on days Mama lay in bed with burning fever while I wasted my days either sleeping or hanging out with Hamza, Anwar, Rana, and the rest. He also helped our neighbours on Fridays by sweeping their houses and yards and feeding their cattle when the menfolk were out of Rahmatpur for business. He hardly accepted the gifts they offered him – lunch, dinner, fresh harvest. When I asked him why he was so keen on helping others, he replied that Allah shows mercy upon those who are merciful to His creations. He is truly a child of God.

People often wrinkled their eyebrows, astonished at how a pair of twins could be so different despite physical similarities.

Every night, under the bulb's yellow haze, Shafi tutored me in maths, English, science, and Qur'an recitation. He could not hold my attention for more than an hour because I would squirm to get out of the house and listen to fictitious djinn stories from our friends instead of learning how to change a sentence from past participle into past perfect, or how fast a tiger needs to be to catch up with a deer, or how to apply *ghunna* and *ikhfa* on Arabic letters. But now I want to move back through time and relive those moments, to be close and attentive to Shafi and his lessons.

A letter or two concerning his whereabouts would have been nice, but the Pakistanis have played havoc with our communication systems and so we scratch our chins and pray for his safety. I personally believe he is safe somewhere out there with his madrasa gang. Or maybe he has fled to India. In that case, even better! My chest puffs with hope when I dream of the day all these evil soldiers drop dead and I get to hug Shafi. My twin whom I love more than Mama (I am sorry, Mama, but he and I swam together inside a womb for nine months... but don't worry, I love you a lot too.) despite his constant badgering—

'Sami, why don't you perform Salah?'

'Sami, aren't you a Muslim? You ought to perform it!'

'Sami, you cannot break your fast like this! It is a major sin.'

'Do you think you can evade the torment of the grave if you keep ignoring your obligations to Allah like this?'

'No, Sami, believing in Allah is not enough. You have to give Him His due!'

He could go on and on and on. He spoke like a fifty-one-year-old man with a long white beard, not a fifteen-year-old boy with a beardless face. Now, to clarify, I am not justifying violating the sanctity of my religion; it's just that my bones are saturated with laziness. In summer, I cannot get out of my bed and go to the washroom to perform *wudu* for praying. In winter, my teeth chitter at the thought of splashing my skin with cold water. I am steaming in sins. Allah help me.

I would be lying if I said I never perform Salah. I perform it three times a day at most instead of five times. I perform it only on days I am overcome with anxiety and sorrow regarding Shafi. I hear satanic whispers that perhaps Shafi is dead. Fatally shot. No, bayoneted. No, abducted and beaten with a stick. No, a bomb blast. Perhaps he is floating on a lake, entangled in a mass of legless, handless, eyeless, headless bodies. And vultures are picking at his flesh. Fish are swimming around his ears. I raise my hands and invoke Allah with tears gathering on my pants. Please, do not let him die. Keep him safe and protected. Grant him ease and wellbeing. My bones ache to sit beside him on the grassy riverbank and listen to him reciting the Qur'an – was it not Surah Rahman that he recited last as we watched egrets and herons take flight across the shimmering river? So please, reunite us. And kill these military monsters.

Mama seals the deal. He prays five times a day. He even prays the night prayer when God descends to the lowest heaven and the entire camp is snoring and the owls are sombrely hooting and the foxes and wolves are howling in the distance as if telling the owls to shut up once and for all because in all honesty their hoots give everyone the creeps. When I wake up to take a leak in the middle of the night, I find it reassuring to see him seated on the prayer mat, muttering verses from the Qur'an, his face caked with dried tears. One night, I woke up to his wailing, which was unusual. He cried, true, but always silently. He was scratching his face, saliva drooping from his face. I wrapped my arms around him, frightened.

'What happened, Mama?'

He couldn't speak. His voice broke whenever he tried.

'Remember how I beat Shafi up because he accidentally broke the new eggs?'

I nodded. The scene floated before me vividly. It had been a Saturday afternoon. Shafi had just got home from the market. He did not notice the polythene bag with the eggs on the porch's stairs as he walked up. Mama had kept them there forgetfully. Shafi tutted as he washed his egg-smelling feet under the tap. 'Who broke the eggs?' Mama screamed, emerging from our giant chicken coop. 'I am sorry, Mama. It was me. I didn't notice,' he said timidly, appearing to shrink into the size of an ant. Mama paced around the porch for a while and ran his hands frantically through his hair. 'How will I buy new ones this week? Do you know how much one has to pay for these? Tell me, do you know?' he continued, screaming. Perhaps Shafi's silence and downward gaze bothered him. Perhaps that's why he took off his pink slipper and thrashed Shafi with it. How Shafi managed to cry silently through this ordeal was beyond me. In the process, he also tore apart the sleeve of Shafi's white thobe.

'That pure, innocent boy. How could I do that to him? How?'

I didn't reply. I just kept holding him as he wailed on, shivering.

One might think Mama is forty. The stress wafting out of Shafi's absence has made his beard grow white patches. He used to possess a muscular build from working at the rice fields from dusk till dawn. But now he is skeletal. Withering from inactivity and consuming scanty meals. He forces himself to eat rice and lentil, but he won't eat more than one meal a day even when I tell him Shafi would not have liked this. Sometimes I joke that he won't get married with a lanky frame like that and he throws me a thin-eyed glance. In those moments, I want to grip his shoulders and jerk a stream of laughter out of him.

It is August. The sun is never out these days. Clouds groan and burst open. Rain strikes the earth and frogs and mongooses scamper for refuge. It has been exactly three months since we left Rahmatpur, Hamza points out to me as we wait with our stomachs growling and our steel bowls out in the long queue for lunch, shivering under the rain. The smoke from the large pot of *khichuri* blends with the wet, earthy smell, sneaking into our noses. It reminds me how Mama would cook *khichuri* for Shafi and me every Friday. If you cooked it for breakfast, lunch, and dinner all year round, Shafi would gobble it up as if he were heavenly offerings.

Years ago, I finished his share of *khichuri* because I thought he would be late and complete his lunch at the mosque where he was busy cleaning with other madrasa folks who had volunteered. He returned right before Maghrib and when he found the steel bowl empty in the kitchen, he went silent for hours. He did not approach to tutor me that night. Neither did he nag me to pray the obligatory Salahs nor did he reply to any of my questions.

After setting up the mosquito net over my cot, I asked him, 'Why are you so quiet? Are you possessed?' I knew very well that he was mad about the *khichuri* theft. The room was dark save for the moonlight cutting through the window and casting a faint glow over the wooden cupboard. If the lights were on, perhaps I could have noticed the rage trembling across his face and dodged his sharp slap. Such behaviour was rare for him. I was frozen with shock. Yes, he would often scold me and shout at me for not studying, not praying my Salahs, not helping with household chores, but that slap felt like an otherworldly event. We didn't speak for a week. Even Mama was upset about the fact that I had caused Shafi distress. Like the generous soul he is, he gifted me a green half-sleeved tunic with white kites embroidered in the middle. The imam at the mosque had gifted it to him for volunteering weekly to clean the mosque. My insides melted in guilt thinking of how he put aside his principle of not taking gifts just to patch things up.

A tear or two left my eyes, and I hugged him. The attar on his neck made him smell like jasmine.

As the rain spatters on and my stomach churns – seriously, does the line only keep growing? – I want to fall asleep and wake up to Shafi's presence. I want to swim in the rain-bloated river back home like Shafi, Hamza, Rana, Anwar and I used to. I want to lie shirtless on the field with our mouths open and taste the fat globs of rain as always. I want to drink tea with them at Sohel Chacha's crowded stall.

Now the clouds grumble with extra ferocity, as though the war has shifted to the sky from land. But wait... I don't think those are clouds. People in the line turn their heads in all directions. Some whisper, some crane their necks. A grey-haired man in a white tunic and maroon lungi emerges from the sloped, narrow road that separates the camp from Kamalpara's houses. He bangs the tents with his black cane and screams: 'Get out all of you! The military is here! Run!'

A moment of disbelief seizes me. How is it possible? Weren't our fighters armed to the teeth and training regularly on the field? The line disbands. Pots and plates bounce and clang on the wet earth. Hamza pulls my collar and I run alongside him. His tent is opposite mine. He goes inside to bring out his mother and sister while I look for Mama. He is at the entrance. 'Where were you?' he says before kissing my cheeks and forehead. He holds my hand tight and runs. Hamza and his family, as many other people, course through the alleyways between the camps. A spell of gunfire cups our ears and rattles our hearts. People are falling behind us. I don't know where the rest of my friends are. I have lost sight of Hamza. I cannot recognize anyone with their frantic cries around me except Mama. We hurry. Beside us, Liaquat Chacha, who is carrying his old hunchbacked mother on his back, is shot in the leg.

When they fall, the woman's cry overpowers her son's. Mama does not bat an eye. I know even if he did, he would not be able to help. We enter a thicket abundantly dotted with hibiscus flowers glowing red. Five minutes into the forest, Mama winces and sits on a fallen tree. He bites on his forearm and brings a bloodied thorn out of his sole. Tears escape his eyes. He heaves. I hug him, my tears mixing with the drops of rain on his hair. 'Listen, Sami. Even if I can't make it, you have to run as far as you can. You understand?' he says, his forehead connected to mine. I nod and rub the snot off my mouth. 'Let's go now. Allah knows how long we need to walk,' he says. I clasp his hand as he limps. The gunfire rages on in the distance, outside the forest. I don't know what will happen to him if the military enters the forest.

We find an abandoned two-storey temple with grimy walls and wild creepers looping around its pillars beside a banyan tree. Mama leaves my hand and says he is going to take a leak behind the bush at the base of the sal tree. As we are about to enter, we hear a cluster of Pakistani soldiers coming from the undergrowth in front of us. We do not get the time to process all this and hide. 'Kill all these devils!' one of them screams and starts showering bullets on us. I am swept by a mass of people running towards the right. I do not go checking for Mama.

I do not know if they have killed him or if he was able to hide or escape somehow. I run with four other people – three young boys and a girl. Bullets ricochet off the trees around us. When the gunshots turn faint and we are reassured that the soldiers cannot catch up with us, we stop to rest and drink from the gurgling creek. I gulp six mouthfuls of water and feel coolness gripping my bones. Magpie robins coo from the trees and invisible frogs croak around us. The heavy rain has turned into a light drizzle. I keep thinking of Mama as I lie on a banana leaf on the ground. He cannot die. I make calculated assumptions: since he was peeing behind the bush, he must have crouched on the ground or run through the trees behind him when the soldiers burst on to the scene. Or did their bullets hit him as he tried to run? Or did they discover him as he remained hiding beneath the bush and bayoneted him to death?

'Look!' the girl screams. We rush to her and see what she sees: around twenty dead bodies – men, women, and children, clothed, half-clothed and unclothed – hanging from the roots of a rain tree. Beneath them is a pit from where we see tips of a few vultures' black and brown flapping wings. We arm ourselves with branches, rocks, and sticks, and go near the pit. 'Hey!' The tallest boy among us shouts at the vultures and strikes his twig on the ground. All the three vultures, their beaks, wings, and talons dripping with blood, take flight. The pit is filled with bodies. Could be twenty. Could be thirty. Some with hands tied. Some with their legs tied. Some without heads. Some without eyes. Some have their bellies open. Some have the lower region of their bodies missing. Wait... is that...? Where did I see that tunic before? My God... it can't be... Isn't that Shafi's tunic? The sky blue one Mama bought for him last Eid? I jump into the pit to turn the body over and check who it really is. Those with me stand open-mouthed at my action and one boy says, 'Hey, boy, what's wrong with you? Have you lost your brain?'

Their complaints become a blur in the distance when I turn the body and see Shafi's face. A thin patch of beard lines his jaw. His eyes are adamantly shut, his lips dark like the wet bark of a tree. His hair is matted with thick blood. There is a hole on his chest. I wonder if the bullet is still in there.

I wonder if he ended up here while fleeing to India. Or did he try to come back to Rahmatpur when the capital was under siege? I rest my head on his chest and let my tears flow into the wound, flies hovering above us. I close my eyes, my hands clasping his cold ones, my legs mingling with the slimy faces and necks of people who once lived.

The cloud starts grumbling. A gust of wind pushes against the trees and brings down leaves. I don't know what the other four are muttering. I don't respond when one of the boys asks, 'Will you please get up? We have to move. We will leave if you don't hurry'.

I cannot believe that here lies my brother. Whose lips will never recite another Surah. Whose fingers will never guide me through geometry and algebra. Whose neck will never smell like jasmine-scented attar. I take my head off his chest and wipe my eyes with my bloodied hands. The left one stings because an eyelash is lodged inside. Tears crowd my eyes again. I can taste their saltiness on my lips. I caress his head for a while. I raise my hands and call out to Allah in silence, with my chest heaving, to reunite me with Shafi in Jannah. I promise Him that I will start praying all my Salahs and reading the Qur'an daily, that I will not let Shafi's annoying persistence be wasted. Fat drops of rain fall on my palms steadily, and very soon, there is a torrent on my hands.

Lucky

Nobody knew what caused Lucky to behave the way she did. Had she come out of the womb too early? Had she fallen off the cot while her aunt was busy washing clothes? Had she bumped into walls a lot? Had she been possessed by a djinn? A long spell of typhoid? Jaundice? Pneumonia? The residents of Niribili scratched their heads but never found answers. They had given up long ago when they tried extracting details from Hamida – Lucky's elder sister by three years – and even she turned out to be clueless. With whatever meagre details they could piece together, they settled on the conclusion that Lucky's behaviour was the river flowing out of the absence of a mother and a poverty-ridden childhood.

She lived in a small tin shed under the banyan tree just outside the tall yellow walls of Niribili, a leafy diplomatic neighbourhood, one of its kind in the city. The kids of Niribili went to the city's only international school. Everywhere you looked, you would find fair-skinned people from foreign countries: a woman in a skirt pushing a pram down the spotless, maroon footpath; a man, AirPods plugged in, jogging by rows of wet tulips and roses in the park; a group of boys and girls dripping with sweat, their sneakers chafing on the concrete as they try to score baskets. You would find that luxury cars – Mercedes, BMW, Audi and Jaguar – were as common here as the Toyota was in other parts of the city. The buildings, arranged in different lanes, ranged from colonial, grime-stricken bungalows to modernist apartment blocks.

Hamida lived and worked as a maid at one of the houses on Lane Seven – a penthouse that provided a view of the entire park. Her employers, both doctors at the same private hospital, had initially given Lucky the opportunity to work at the penthouse and live with them despite her tendency to scar the people around her by hurling at them random and hideous scenarios and accusations.

'Tell your father I saw him in a dream. His mistress sliced him in half when she discovered he is married!' she would very often say to an unfortunate individual who happened to be around her, before exploding into a high-pitched laughter. To another, she would say, 'If I see you doing *naughty-naughty* with your madam again, I swear I will feed you my slipper!' and take off her slipper, wiggling it threateningly. To another, she would say, 'Did you eat the black dog you caught yesterday? Was it cooked okay?' as her forehead flaunted wavy lines.

Once, she said to the aged caretaker of the building, 'I am sorry that your daughter drowned. I hope she is in heaven.' Fearing for the safety of his daughter, he sprinted inside his room in the garage, called home while rubbing his eyes, and told her to stay away from all the water bodies in his village. He had left that evening for his village and never returned. Another time, she said to a ten-year-old girl who was parking her blue four-wheeled cycle by the grey electric pole, 'How is your baby? Are you feeding her well? And your husband? Feeding him well too? Is your mother-in-law beating you too much?' Tears bloomed in her eyes. Her lips wrinkled and trembled. Lucky embraced her seeing her on wail, and said,

'Don't you worry, darling. I will teach your in-laws a lesson.' She wailed louder upon hearing this.

Because she avoided the foreigners as though even looking at them would cause her death, only the locals fidgeted at Lucky's presence. Nobody knew when they would be accused of engaging in black magic, adultery, incest, Satan-worshipping, extramarital affairs, murder and robbery (the list was endless).

The employers fired her when she slapped one of their two fifteen-year-old boys in front of their American, Indian and Japanese friends in the living room without the slightest provocation. He looked at her in horror and disbelief, his hand clutching at his hot cheek. She sighed in relief, clasping her hands together, and said, 'Okay, now you can continue talking with your friends. The djinn inside you is gone! That sly thing. How dare he smirk at me!'

They were kind enough to buy a ticket en route to Sylhet for her. But she refused. Instead, she asked them to build a tin shed for her under the Banyan tree outside Niribili so that she could meet Hamida regularly and live with the birds, dogs, cats, owls, bats and monkeys. Hamida protested at the prospect of her sister rotting out there. She pinched her eyebrows, standing in front of the shed with its two windows and an attached bathroom. How would her shed handle heavy rains? Wouldn't she be cooked in the afternoon heat? Wouldn't the mosquitoes from the trees and shrubs around fatten themselves with her blood? Lucky crossed her arms like an indignant child and refused to budge. She would weather it all, but she would not step out of her new home.

'Don't you see the fan? It will keep me cool all day,' she said, pointing at the sky blue exhaust fan fitted above the rusty silver trunk, when Hamida bought her lunch on the first day after moving in. 'And these scoundrel mosquitoes can't harm me either. I have this mosquito net. Look... there. See? Happy now?' she added, swatting at her skeletal leg.

Owing to an avalanche of complaints, when the authority had banned her entry, she threatened to stab herself at the gate and terrorize the people even more. After much contemplation with the board members, the man in charge decided to let her in once every week on religious grounds. 'If we do not show mercy to Allah's creation, He won't be merciful towards us,' he had said in the committee meeting.

Hamida's heart rattled in anticipation on the days Lucky did not visit Niribili. Every evening, after Asr prayer, she would check in on Lucky at the shed. She did not find her there most of the time. So, she waited until the Maghrib azan split through the evening sky coloured by strokes of lavender and flame and watched birds shoot towards home and cars *honk-honk-honk* their way inside and outside the neighbourhood at the rush hour. Even after the last birds disappeared and the echoes of azan vanished into the temporary evening coolness, Lucky did not return. On those rare occasions when she did find her napping at the shed or breaking peanut shells with determination and collecting them in a plastic bowl, she would ask her, 'Why can't I ever find you here? Where do you go? Tell me and I will try meeting you there.' To which Lucky would reply with a coarse laughter, 'I walk a great distance from here to meet my friends. Your Sir and Madam will never allow you to leave work and go that far. Just stop worrying about me. Be happy that you get to see me once every week at least!' It was a repetitive conversation, one that always felt new owing to Hamida's frustration stemming from Lucky's absence. Her mind had become a boiling cauldron of anxiety.

The rogue types could violate Lucky. Didn't they gang rape a mentally challenged women the other day in Badda? A drunk driver's truck could flatten her. Her corpse could languish in a derelict morgue with no one caring to contact her relatives. She could suffer a sudden stroke and lay dead in a ditch far away, her body waiting to be feasted on by stray dogs and boars. She could go so far that she could not find her way back. She could get trafficked into sex slavery. She could be forced into begging after her legs are hacked off and her eyes gouged out.

On the days she visited Niribili, Hamida carefully inspected Lucky's body, checking for bruises and cuts. She had her undress inside her room at the penthouse for the investigation. She prayed extra two *rakah* voluntary prayers thanking Allah for protecting her and begging Him to continue doing so. 'The next time you do it, I will throw you from the veranda, you understand?' Hamida would say at the end of the weekly inspections, adjusting her *orna* over her shoulder. She knew her words were weightless in the face of Lucky's steely determination. She never obeyed Hamida; surely, she could offer a concession in this one case. A year later, Hamida's tensions abated, and she stopped the inspections.

On the first Sunday of December, Lucky had her first physical fight in the neighbourhood. The midday sun had chased away the fog. The sweeper lady was dusting the rusty leaves off the road in front of Hamida's employers' house. Lucky was exiting the building, jubilant for no particular reason. On noticing the lady, she said, 'Tch Tch. You have gained so much weight! Are you carrying a hippo's flesh inside?' The lady's nostrils flared, and because she was cranky that day owing to the fact that her son had to be admitted to the hospital on account of yet another alcohol poisoning event, she pounded on Lucky with her bamboo broom. She sat on Lucky's belly and hammered sharp blows on her face with the uneven end of her broom. The passers-by watched open-mouthed. Lucky's shrieks sounded like a mongoose being hacked to death. That frightening noise climbed the air all the way up to the kitchen where Hamida was scaling a Hilsa fish. She dropped the fish on the steel bowl, washed her hands quickly and looked out the gigantic kitchen window. 'Hey! Hey! You devil! Stop it! I will slit your throat if you don't!' she shouted before dashing out the door and down the stairs barefoot. By the time she reached the scene, her employers' driver was able to stop the fight. He held back a growling and groaning Lucky, her face marinated in blood. She strove to break free and launch herself on the lady. A group of other sweeper ladies escorted their colleague away while she adjusted her headscarf and fumed. Later, the ladies, allied with their entire workforce, complained to the Niribili authority that they demanded the complete absence of Lucky in the neighbourhood; otherwise, they would wage a strike for harassment. In the course of a week, it was decided that Lucky was never to set foot in the neighbourhood. Hamida thought of begging her employers to protest, but even she was tired of having to let Lucky be herself. After all, she could not blame someone if they, like that lady, beat Lucky up for her crass statements. She decided that the ban was for the best. If it had not been imposed, perhaps Lucky would have to fall into more violent episodes, which would not only inflict dark red scars and blueish bruises on her face but also cause her to live with a broken spine, a fractured arm, or a shattered jaw.

By the end of December, Lucky grew a habit of walking with her dogs (three of the many she had befriended over the course of her stay at the shed) in the evenings around the outer perimeters of Niribili. She plucked sunflowers and roses from the long stretch of garden skirting the walls and put them behind her dogs' ears. Some she lodged underneath her pink bangles with a thread. She carried a few bananas in her tote bag which she had found in the narrow canal opposite to her shed. She peeled and left them on the roadside for the monkeys that migrated en masse from one forest to another through the driveway leading to Niribili's main gate.

With the new habit seeped into her, she did not miss terrorising the people of Niribili. Their memory was a stain she had wiped off her skin. Except two maids and Hamida, no one from the neighbourhood cared enough to regularly check up on her. She had her old-time friends – women as old as seventy and girls as young as nine. They lived under the foot overbridge on the main road and inside flimsy huts with hole-bearing tarpaulins beside the snaking rail-line. She walked long distances and sang and played tag and hide-and-seek at the sprawling construction site by the river with them (on the days she did not walk with her dogs). At least three days a week, she joined them in singing and scavenging plastic in the middle of the night from the ghostly quiet roads. And the times they got too high from sniffing glue to find their way home, she escorted them, all the while rapidly shaking her head at their persistent proposals to try some.

It was just after Fajr prayer. Dawn had not completely broken yet. The sky was a dim blue ocean, sagging with the cawing of crows and the singing of mynahs, parakeets, and cuckoos. A soft breeze caressed the walls, the steel fence, the red swings, the yellow slides, the soldier-like jackfruit trees, and Lucky's shampooed hair. It had been months since she had last shampooed her hair. If not for the maid from the pharmaceutical mogul's house, who often stopped by her shed and chatted late into the night after her shift, she would have gone on for more months. The breeze in her hair reminded her of Hamida: the way she would stroke Lucky's long hair before massaging with warm oil every winter night, back when Lucky lived in the Lane Seven penthouse.

Lucky followed Kaali, one of her dogs, as he inspected a dead mouse on the walkway. She bent down and ruffled his black, furry ears. 'Tch, don't bother with it. Come here,' she said, walking towards Laali, another one of her dogs, who was panting near the moss-strewn wall having just urinated.

Before she could reach Laali, a black Audi SUV drove between them, smashing Laali's skull beneath its tires. The car paused for a while. But once Laali's cries and Lucky's screams mingled into a grim song, it sped away, leaving bloodied tracks on the driveaway. She raced towards Laali, a brownish-orange, fluffy mass leaking dark blood, squeaking, whimpering. She held her in her arms and cried gibberish into her ears. Her blood coated Lucky's salwar kameez, hands, and face with the warmth of a life departing. Around them, Kaali frantically paced about and let out fierce screams like a wolf calling out to its pack.

*

In the tragedy's wake, Lucky gave up speaking and picked up barking – shrill, low-pitched, trying her best to capture Laali's essence. Her hair grew matted and woolly. She stopped having showers. She wore the same blood-stained salwar kameez every day, as if to never part with Laali completely.

If somebody crossed paths with her, they pinched their noses in disgust without facing any consequences. Normally, she would have scoffed at them and threatened to pelt stones in reply. Now she would simply bark, and they would stare in disbelief before hurrying out of her sight. She did not walk long distances anymore. She no longer spoke to passers-by, only responded with barks to their queries. She remained seated in her shed. She drank tea on its steps and gazed at the gurgling canal on the other side. She spent hours staring at the creepers climbing up the rain-tree on the canal's bank.

When the maid from the only bungalow on Lane Nine asked what happened, she turned to the other side and pretended to fall asleep after letting out a stream of barks. The woman squinted, as if to gauge whether she was Lucky or one of her aloof friends. When the maid from the pharmaceutical company CEO's house did the same, Lucky not only barked but also went so far as to bite her. 'Ei, ei, stop it, you witch! I will hang your dead body from that tree if you come closer,' the woman said while panting and retreating.

When Hamida visited and asked how things were with her, Lucky clutched her in a hug and cried for as long as ten minutes. The dried blood stains on her clothes pulled open Hamida's mouth. 'Who did this to you? Please, sister, tell me who did this to you? What happened to you?' She jerked Lucky back and forth to wring out an answer. Lucky barked continuously in reply, which made Hamida glare. Her eyes threatened to grow bigger than her face. 'What are you doing, Lucky? Please, stop! Please, please!' she wailed. But Lucky did not stop. Hamida distanced herself from Lucky until her back was to the wall. Her hands wrapped around her knees, she stayed sitting. She cried and covered her ears watching Lucky bark.

Hamida's heaving cries slowed to a faint whimper. She charged out of her position and dragged Lucky to the bathroom despite her screams. Lucky bit Hamida's finger. She slapped Lucky so hard that she fell on the ground. Now, she barked with more energy, like a dog spotting a thief. Once inside, she poured water from the bucket over Lucky. She undressed a shivering Lucky, inspected her body, and found no signs of assault. 'Where did the stains come from? Tell me! You have to tell me today. I cannot tolerate your stupidity anymore. You think you can have your way every time? What do you think of yourself?' Hamida screamed.

Lucky's face was downwards. Her barking subdued, now sounding more like a rat's squeaking. Still screaming, Hamida picked up the bucket and hovered it for a while over Lucky, wanting to smash her head, wanting to end the root of all her tensions. She threw the bucket out the bathroom door and it knocked the waist-level garbage bin over. Without looking back at Lucky, Hamida stormed out, wiping her face in vain because the tears seemed as endless as Lucky's illness.

She wanted her sister's illness gone and to exhale a long breath of relief. But Lucky and her condition were as inseparable as a beating heart and a stream of blood. So Hamida's wish involuntarily translated into wishing her sister gone. As she walked home, the air from cars whooshing past making her wet body shiver, she winced at the thought.

How could she crave her absence? Her baby sister whom she taught swimming in the lake with coconuts and banana plants back at their village in Sylhet. Whom she gave an extra bite from her share of food whenever a rich family in the village hosted feasts. Whom she defended from their raging aunt whose hatred for Lucky showed in the pulsating veins in her forearms. Whom she sang lullabies to at night, praying for the jagged bruises (from the beating Lucky had incurred from their aunt's metallic cooking spud on her legs) to heal quickly.

Whom she tried to protect from the kids who threw berries, apples, stones and rocks by pelting those things back at them. Whom she freed from the locked hut behind the *kashphool* field by hacking at the door with a machete as their aunt and her accomplices negotiated the rate of selling Lucky. Whom she brought to the city on a train's mist-covered rooftop to begin their lives anew.

Meanwhile, Lucky's name garnered a new, lively reputation in Niribili on account of her recent transformation. Cleaners, drivers, maids, shopkeepers, caretakers, and even groups of curious residents milled around Lucky's shed. Hands on their bellies, they laughed as Lucky barked. When her barks were loud, the laughter would grow loud as well. And when she did not bark, they would throw rocks at her shed, trying to elicit a response from her. The men were specifically lewd. They imitated her barking, and it soon gave way to suggestive moaning. They stuck out their tongues, bit their lips and stroked their chests. From morning till evening, the spectacle went on every day with the same undying energy. It made Lucky look as though she were a chimpanzee at a zoo entertaining its visitors.

Hamida had to bear the brunt of Lucky's new avatar as well. The caretaker of her building barked and laughed out loud every time she passed by him. Her employers' driver called her 'the white dog' since her complexion was fairer than Lucky's. The garbage truck's driver often joked while tilting his head towards the green tailgate, 'Did you find your sister in there? Lots of dogs sniff through the things. Look carefully, you might find her.' Nearly all the maids on Lane Seven avoided her and barked in unison if a group of them happened to see Hamida on the road. The caretakers from other lanes who walked their owners' dogs said to their

German Shepherds, Golden Retrievers and Pomeranians, 'Look, look, there goes your sister!' Hamida was angry not only at those who enjoyed the misery of her family but also at Lucky. She could not digest the fact that Lucky had made her life intolerable to this extent. She found it unfair that Lucky's problems now defined her, which was why she did not visit her after her transformation. She was not sure whether she would finally end up smashing her head with the bucket if she heard her barking again instead of replying properly to her questions.

A week after the change, Hamida decided to call the Army-run mental hospital near the airport, like her employers had suggested on hearing about Lucky. With a generous donation from them and a portion of Hamida's income, Lucky would be well accounted for. She cooked *khichuri* and chicken curry – dense, spicy, like Lucky preferred it. Before the afternoon prayer, she went to Lucky's shed and fed her. This time, Lucky was so engrossed in eating her favourite meal that she did not bark at those who were calling out to her, barking, moaning, throwing stones, desperate for their daily dose of entertainment. The tin walls protected them from the world outside.

Lucky gobbled up every morsel as though it were the last meal of her life. The childlike energy dancing across her eyes made Hamida tear up. She pushed aside the tears with the end of her *orna*. They still rolled down her face. Her lips trembled. She wanted to say that she loved her dearly, that she was sorry for being mad at her, that it was not Lucky's fault that she had turned out like this.

When she tried to speak, her voice broke. She wailed into the crook of her arms. Lucky did not mind her. She took it upon herself to finish the meal now. As she ate, Hamida stroked Lucky's hair and shoulders with her left hand. 'I love you a lot, my sister. A lot,' she said, cleaning the snot from her face. Lucky, as expected, did not reply. She was busy tearing the chicken's breast, her hands soaked in yellow curry.

Outside, a siren blared. Hamida heard the crunch of tires pulling up near the shed.

The people from the mental hospital were here. She went out the door and asked them to wait a while. The people looking for entertainment were muttering among themselves, confusion lashing at their faces.

After Lucky finished the meal, Hamida poured water over her hands and wiped her mouth. She kissed her forehead, her cheeks. She hugged and sniffed her. Lucky now barked. Not in an aggressive manner but like a puppy when it licks its mother.

Hamida asked the people to come inside. A lady and two men in sky blue scrubs gently held Lucky and took her towards the white Hiace. But once outside, she dug her feet into the ground and twirled, her hair stinging their eyes. She let out loud barks and bit one of the men's arm. The lady pinned her to the ground. Lucky writhed and spat when her teeth could not reach the lady. A wave of whistles and shouts wafted from the onlookers who were, finally, seeing yet another Lucky-related spectacle. Another man brought a needle from the microbus and jabbed it into her neck. The lady got off of Lucky, dusting her uniform. Lucky's writhing continued for a while, and then she lay motionless, her hair and salwar kameez crusted with mud.

The Hippo Girl

Jhonaki's obsession with the hippos started after her parents' deaths. It was as if grief didn't want to enter her body, so it gently stepped aside and made way for the obsession to settle instead.

If she wasn't playing tag with us at the abandoned Neelkuthi the day her parents died, she would have died too. Her father had not been able to sell his crops in the market for close to seven months. The land where he grew his crops had turned infertile. No one really knew why. The plots beside that land, however, were flourishing. The landowner blamed his poor farming techniques for the long spell of loss. The family was living off borrowed money from the landowner. They could have sought their relatives' help if the relatives themselves were rich enough. Looking to the landlords, as everyone here knows, is like hanging yourself from the highest branch of a banyan tree. When the landowner's kindness ran out and he threatened to chase the family out of the village, her father turned to his useless sickle. And hacked her mother to death. Then, slashed his own throat.

We realized Jhonaki wasn't okay when relatives and friends of the two were simmering with sorrow but not a single tear rolled out of her eyes. Instead, she emptily stared at the bodies lying in pools of dark blood on the earthen floor, walked towards the big mound of hay beneath the neem tree where the one-eared hippo was snoozing, settled herself cosily against its wet belly, and like a baby in its mother's embrace, fell asleep.

Our mouths hung open at the spectacle. Everyone in the village knew how terrible it was to even touch these beasts. We grew up hearing stories from our elders about how these beasts were embodiments of evil left by the British all those years ago. They told us that the white men brought these fat, filthy animals from faraway lands and 'let them breed like rabbits here'. They told us how, on account of the white men mercilessly oppressing and killing our people, the villagers started associating the hippos with the memories of those dark years and accordingly, avoided interactions with them. The only interaction included shooing them away with sticks and twigs when they got too close to their lands, threatening to walk all over the fresh crops. Sometimes, if the villagers were a little careless, the hippos, jumping at the chance, would eat half a row of pumpkins or rice stalks. The villagers would then hit them with stones and chase them away. But the villagers never dared to kill them, the elders told us, because no one knew what these beasts held inside their bellies, what ominous thing could rush forth from their insides and haunt the village for generations like the white men did. Moreover, so far, the hippos have not killed anyone, which Mr Gupta, our science teacher, found very confusing. As he told us, hippos were supposed to be deadly. In Africa, where they were originally from, they smashed people's skulls between their sharp yellow teeth.

But the reality in our village was different. The hippos milled about the school compound, the temple, the mosque, the ghostly mansions overrun by weeds and creepers, the sprawling market, the field near the collector's office, grazed at the *kashphool* fields alongside the cows and the sheep, wallowed in the river, lay on the sandy bank, soaking in the sun, moaning, grunting and snorting.

They minded their own business, which was why everyone decided coexistence was the best way to preserve the peace of this place.

After the incident, our parents told us to maintain a distance from Jhonaki. Even her khala, who chose to take her in, didn't let her stay inside her house. She had a small shed with nets and fences built beside the chicken coop for Jhonaki. Slowly, everyone in the village stopped batting their eyes about her. They let her be as she rode the one-eared hippo and toured the entire village almost regularly.

At that time, we were in the fifth grade. No one sat beside her. She smelled of mud, dung and river. She stopped coming to the fields in the afternoons to play marbles, tag and hide-and-seek with us like before. We often found her covered in mud and sand on the riverbank, lying beside the one-eared hippo as the other hippos rolled and bounced and paced around them as if they were the throne-holders of that hippo kingdom.

When her khala said she could not pay for her schooling, given she had three boys of her own to educate, our principal ma'am was kind enough to allow Jhonaki to continue her education even though her school fees hadn't been paid for the last seven months on account of her father's failing crops.

Every month, she called Jhonaki into her room. We did not know why she called her in with that kind of regularity. So, we pressed our ears to the wooden door, eavesdropping. It turned out that she was failing the monthly class tests. We chuckled because why wouldn't she. Didn't she fall asleep in class while we were being taught about gravity, multiplication, tenses, Bangla grammar, and Jibanananda Das' poetry?

It rained all morning on the result day as if to fit the anticipation roiling inside our ribs. At school, some of us were being cuffed on the ears by our parents, some of us were being shouted at, some of us were being patted on our shoulders. A little after the rains abated, we saw Jhonaki run out of principal ma'am's room, ignoring her calls, galloping across the compound and out the rusty metal gate. Later, we learned that she had failed the final exams (out of hundred, twelve in math, five in science, two in English, four in Bangla, nine in social studies, seven in religious studies) and decided to sacrifice her education to spend all her time with the one-eared hippo.

She would be in the ninth grade, like we are now, if she hadn't taken such a foolish decision. We are pretty sure though that her love for the one-eared hippo – all the hippos of our village, in general – has blinded her from reasoning with herself. Like when you shoot your gaze directly at the sun and are blinded.

Bags heavy on our shoulders, the sun merciless against our skin, we trudge towards home. Around us, the rice-fields and the palm trees are still. We can feel the earth simmering beneath our shoes. The heat is so terrible that even the hippos aren't strolling around on land. Their snorts ride the hot air and reach us all the way from the riverbank. A herd of egrets whooshes past us, a brief gust of wind lapping at our bodies.

As we take a turn towards the alley after crossing Rehmat's *paan* shop, we see Jhonaki licking an orange lolly, her eyes closed, her hands firmly clasping the rings of fat around the one-eared hippo's head. The hippo is walking down the alley, towards us, chewing a long and thick bundle of grass. This is the first time we have seen her in a week. Our gaze meets hers. She stares at us but does not say anything. We keep looking at her as she, straddled on the hippo, crosses us. Her belly is protruded, as if she is hiding a coconut inside her red frock. Her face appears fleshier than before. Our eyebrows crawl in confusion.

The next day, at school, everyone is talking about it. Jhonaki's pregnancy.

'Who did that?'

'I have never seen a man anywhere near her.'

'She lives in that shed at her aunt's, no? Do you think maybe it was her uncle?'

'What rubbish!'

'The labourers from the construction site?'

'Does she have an affair though? Could it be related to that?'

'I don't know. She is pretty dumb, isn't she? She doesn't speak, spends all her time with the beasts day and night. I don't think she is involved in those things.'

'You know, you can never predict anything about abnormal people like her. I mean, she is only fifteen and look what she is up to! First, the hippos and now this.'

To the village, the news is a shock. The fact that she is pregnant has surpassed our wildest imagination. She could have disappeared from the village one day without notice, for all we care. And still, that would not match the severity of the current situation.

In the evening, the elders call for a meeting on the imam's porch, where meetings concerning common and uncommon village affairs usually take place. They seem to think that someone must have taken advantage of her. Jhonaki's aunt cries like she has an endless stock of tears. Her dark headscarf turns sleek in the lantern's glow.

'How will I feed another mouth? My husband is a barber, for god's sake! It's not fair. How can someone just take advantage of my dumb niece and get away with it? I beg of you, bhaijaan, please find the cruel man and ask him to marry her and relieve us of the trouble!'

'Don't worry, Hamida apa. Be rest assured that all of us – the financially suitable villagers, that is – will chip in with whatever amount we can, should the culprit not be found anytime soon.'

'What do you mean? Do you think this poor, brainless girl and the baby can live off your mercy for a long time? And what about my children? How am I going to feed them once this baby comes?'

'Apa, we understand your concerns, but you tell us, what can we do?'

She grinds her teeth, pulls her fingers, and storms off, fuming. A mob of hippos burps and growls, chewing grass and hay a few steps away from the imam's house.

The news of the pregnancy still fresh and alive on every tongue, another news fans out with the dawn. Jhonaki has been kicked out of the shed. We aren't worried about where she will stay though. As usual, we will spot her – but even more now – on the riverbank with her hippo. By the huge mounds of hay, at times. The empty fields, the *kashphool* groves.

At school, our classmates and friends talk about how their parents are thinking of donating food and old clothes to her from time to time. They speculate whether her child would turn out to be abnormal like her. Would it be dark-skinned like her or a milky white thing like her mother? They joke that the child would turn out to be a chatterbox, as opposed to her silent nature. And then she would grow so frustrated with it that she would spend more time with her beloved hippos than her own blood, that she would be more interested in swatting buzzing flies away from her hippos' faces than the child's.

After school breaks, we stumble upon a commotion near the landlord's house. The landlord's wife, Zulekha, is on a wooden stretcher, squirming, wailing, a thick wad of brown cloth pressed around her left leg. It seems that there's no leg, only gushing blood. Her hair is clumped, pressed onto her head, sticky with sweat. Two men lift the stretcher and place it on the bullock cart. The landlord hurriedly mounts the cart and shouts at the thick-set man in charge of the cart, 'Who are you waiting for? Quick!' The cart drives off.

We dart inside the gate and find Jhonaki's one-eared hippo lying on the ground beside the well. Five men take turns hacking at it with their long machetes. They grunt after each blow. The hippo, on the other hand, is silent. We wonder if it has died already.

The guard is drinking lemonade from a metallic cup under the mango tree. We ask him what happened.

'She was fetching bananas from the orchard,' he says before taking a drag, 'when the sly hippo showed up from behind and bit her leg off.'

We are frozen with fear. It is as if someone has stuffed us up with ice blocks. We imagine Mr Gupta sighing in relief at the fact that his words have finally turned true – hippos indeed gobble up humans.

The men wipe the sweat off their foreheads with their bloodied sleeves. The hippo's fat body makes their strikes bounce. Blood is oozing out of its body, widening the pool around it, darkening the grass. Moments later, the blood crawls towards our feet. We have Bangla, English, and math homework due tomorrow. At this point, we aren't bothered by the fact. We fix our eyes at the machetes swishing up and coming down. We look around and cannot find Jhonaki anywhere.

Panic has fallen over the village like a stubborn stain. The streets, the stalls, the fields, the orchards and the playgrounds are empty. Men have stopped going to the mosque for prayers. The temple has been emptied of its usual bustle. Our parents won't let us out. Our fathers and elder brothers, especially, are guarding the houses with sticks in their hands. They are shooing away any hippo that approaches. Kids spray them with stones. They moan and run away. The silence of the village has made way for the hippos' noises to thrive in the air. We desperately want to go outside and play football. We think our parents are being foolish. It was just one hippo who attacked Zulekha. That doesn't mean every other hippo will do the same.

By the grace of God, the panic lasts for three days only. Everyone in the village can be seen walking with a long stick now. Even the kids. They have turned this new reality into a plaything. They're using the sticks like guns, pretending to be soldiers at war. At times, they're even striking one another out of playfulness.

When we play football, some of us stand as guards with our sticks around the field. We take turns every day to ensure fairness. It's extremely frustrating to keep watch for any potentially harmful hippos and miss out on the fun of playing. The players' shouts and cackles dancing in the afternoon breeze don't help much. We get the urge to abandon this scheme of guarding, but we are also afraid of losing our hands or legs, or worse, our lives. So that's a fair sacrifice we ought to make. We make prayers to God daily so that He makes the hippos vanish from our village one day.

*

No one has seen Jhonaki recently. Not on the riverbank, on any of the hippos' backs, not around the orchards, the groves.

We have just performed the Jummah prayer and are buying *jhaalmuri* from the old lady at the market when Jhonaki appears with a shiny dagger in her hand. With light steps, she approaches the landlord who is inspecting the brown and black chickens' legs and necks. In the blink of an eye, she plunges it into the landlord's back.

'This is for my friend, you monster,' she says, her eyes sparkling with sinister light.

Our hearts drop. Our bones rattle. We tighten our grip around our sticks in fear.

The landlord gasps for breath and groans, falling over the counter filled with meat. Arzu, the short woman in charge of that stall, screams.

This is the first time we have heard Jhonaki speak in a long time. The childish thinness of her voice is still there. Her belly has swollen more than before. So has the fleshiness of her face. She is wearing a blue gown smeared with patches of clay, mud and thick blades of grass. She looks as though she has been living under the earth for months and has emerged now for a change of air.

The landlords' bodyguards, who, until the attack, were busy drinking juice three stalls beside the landlord, are now charging at her. She doesn't run. We wonder if she could run with that big belly if she chose to. They beat her with their sticks together. She cackles delightfully. She doesn't wince. Her dusty and bloodied face beams with a sense of achievement. Her cackles soon trickle to moans. Then coughs. Then silence.

*

The heavens have opened. Lavender lighting strikes the horizon intermittently, painting everything bright for a split second. Our thatch roofs *thak-thak-thak* against the raging rains. After we have completed our dinner (*khichuri* with beef bhuna, courtesy of the rain) and tucked ourselves into our woolly blankets with animal prints, we feel our cots tremble. The walls, the ground, the jugs, the glasses, too, begin trembling soon. We look out the window and cannot make out what it is amid the dark. But we can surely sense something – like a cluster of boulders – hurtling from the horizon. Our mothers hastily put medicines, biscuits and clothes into polythene bags. Our fathers grab the savings from the rusty trunks under our cots and throw them into a jute sack. We pace around our houses, deciding whether we should start running now. Will we hold any chance if the cyclone strikes quicker than we can think?

A series of lighting reveals before us that we don't have to worry about a cyclone. It is the hippos who are charging. All together. We have never seen them together. And to think that they are united and raging closer with every passing second is enough to make us soil ourselves.

With bags and sacks slung over our shoulders, we rush out of our houses and keep running towards no direction in particular.

A man shouts, 'O, look! Isn't that Jhonaki on the hippo?' A woman replies, 'What? Has the devil swallowed your head?'

Some climb the swaying trees, assuming the forms of flailing fruits. Some hit rocks and tin roofs and fall on the ground, moaning and trying to stop the blood spurting out of their limbs. Some succumb under the weight of their belongings on their backs and heads. Some get buried under the endless stream of running feet. Reena Aunty, the sweeper from our school, is one of them.

Around us, cries mingle with the rain. We do not look back. We can feel the hippos' heavy footsteps come closer and closer, on the verge of overtaking us. We hear the houses behind us getting rammed by their force, tin, thatch, wood and bamboo being crushed under their feet.

Our hearts wobble, start melting almost. The hippos' grunts envelope our ears like warm palms.

We do not look back. We run and then just keep on running.

A Blazing History of Rage

Sometimes we think our father is hell-bent on shipping us off to a cadet college because we do not have a mother and the weight of this responsibility wilts his shoulders. If she were still breathing, after the doctors prised her belly open and plucked me and Sohel out, perhaps he would not be so obsessed.

When we got promoted to the sixth grade, he enrolled us at a coaching centre in Mirpur that sits right on the chaotic and dust-battered main road. Earlier, he would only emit flimsy tufts of declarations about preparing us for cadet college admission and harp about admitting us to a coaching centre for that purpose.

'Just imagine the life you two would have!' he would say before taking a sip of his morning tea, his face beaming with high hopes. Seated on the breakfast table, scrambled eggs steaming before us, Sohel and I would throw each other impassive looks.

At times, such as when getting ready for school in a hurry after waking up late, he would say, 'In a cadet college, this won't be allowed, you know that? They will wake you up very early and make you take showers even during winter.'

At times, such as when eating with our bare hands at a restaurant, he would smirk and say, 'Such unsmart manners are not tolerated in cadet college. They make you eat with cutlery all the time.'

At times, such as when a sleek army jeep stood beside our car during the afternoon traffic on Satmasjid road, he would give a gentle nudge to my elbow or Sohel's, depending on who sat beside him, and say, 'Do you know it becomes very easy to get into the army, navy, or air force if you are a cadet college graduate?'

His attitude did not ruffle our faces back then. Sohel and I simply brushed it aside thinking he was just being stern with us because of our constant bad grades in school. But the day he took us to the coaching centre's main office and spoke to the head teacher – a clean-shaven, plump man with fluffy grey hair and thick layers of cologne – the impending reality hit us like it was an unruly truck ploughing into pedestrians on a footpath.

That event cleaved our life into two main episodes – a Before and an After. In the Before, our father had a short temper, true, but it was not as bad as it was now. Yes, he would scold us and threaten to stop paying our school fees and cuff us on the ears and sink his fingers into our thin arms and thump us on the shoulders whenever we got less than seventy per cent in the mid and final term exams (especially in math, science and Bangla). But now, in the After, he does all of these – with an extra fist of intensity – every damn week when the weekly test results from the coaching centre light up not only his Samsung but also his rage. In every punch he lands on our arms, in every slap that jolts our cheeks, in every pull of the sideburns, we feel desperation coursing through his being. He really wants to send us away.

Last week, he scolded and beat us in the car all the way home from the coaching centre. The unrelenting traffic made the experience more horrible, as if the cars and buses and trucks and rickshaws on the road had conspired to coil around us and prolong our agony. Most of the slaps reached Sohel's cheeks, thankfully, because he had failed in the weekly math test. I had not failed, but his pinches reminded me I had not scored decent either (five out of twenty). It was embarrassing to have our ageing driver uncle witness all this. We wondered what he thought. Did he ever treat his kids the same way? Does his heart soften out of pity towards us? After we reached home, his rage subsided but he did not speak to us until a day later.

This is how it works – on the weekly test result days, there are lots of beating and scolding followed by a spell of silence and days of normalcy until another set of results pops up. On those days, Sohel and I steady our positions at the centre's collapsible gate and shoot our glances on the road to spot our silver Corolla from a sea of Corollas and Hyundais and Noahs and Premios. Once we spot it, we run, past tea and *paan* stalls, past sleeping dogs, past *jhaalmuri* sellers, past a row of parked motorbikes. Sometimes cough and *paan* stains leap on our legs in the process. But we do not care because one of us needs the front seat which is like a sanctuary; after all, sitting there offers protection from the vigorous beating the one sitting beside our father would receive. Relief shrouds our limbs the times we notice that due to being stuck with work at the hospital he is not in the car.

*

After licking the plates clean, we are supposed to throw the chicken bones into the yellow bin under the kitchen sink and wash the plates. Then we are supposed to solve a chapter of around thirty square root divisions for the test at the coaching centre tomorrow. But our computer table seems to grow wooden hands and zigzag out of the room and into the kitchen, tapping our heads. So, we quickly wash our hands without handwash, our fingers yellow around the edges and sprint to play *Just Cause: 2*.

When the calling bell startles us, we jump off the chairs and pretend that we have just finished our dinner so that father does not suspect our intentional delaying. Father is speaking on the phone with a friend while untying the knot of his green tie. One of his legs is on the sofa, his face towards the window. Golden lights from the hurrying cars on the road glimmer on the black endpieces of his glasses. His hearty laughter pricks us from head to toe. We do not understand why he cannot be like that with us. We believe his obsession with our grades and cadet college has kicked out love from his heart, like the crows we watched that day chasing away a sparrow up in the jackfruit tree.

We turn our gaze from him and walk into the room. It was father's grand idea to have us share a room. There are two single beds, the computer desk in between. We must give him credit for getting at least one thing in our favour. Opposite the beds are our study desks. Sohel's bed overlooks a patch of wooded area with a single tin house. Every morning, parakeets, warblers, sparrows, mynahs, magpies and crows split the air with sharp calls.

Our fingers itch to turn on the monitor and resume playing the mission where we are required to jump off a helicopter into a lush green forest full of coconut and palm trees.

The stupid math book with its stupid bottle green colour begs us to be opened. We run our eyes through the problems but cannot solve most of them. There is a thick guidebook which we do not use since our eyes threaten to retreat into their sockets seeing all the solutions on the pages waiting to be swallowed one by one. We tried memorizing them a few times but still failed as they vaporized out of our heads by the time we sat down for the tests.

The preparation for cadet college admissions is based on the seventh grade, and we barely listen to the teachers in the coaching classes. So how can a guidebook save us? We play tic-tac-toe on the last page of our copies with the three friends we have made there. We whip out our PSPs and Nintendos, lower the volume and play GTA or *Dragon Ball Z*, hiding our hands and devices under the rusty desks. We play rock-paper-scissors. We clasp our fingers and play thumb wrestling. We stare at the white board without purpose as literature passages and algebraic equations run riot over it.

*

At school, I am a *hijra* because Sohel – back in the fourth grade – cried when a teacher threatened to call our father as he had been late to enter the class after the tiffin period. His crying made the other kids bestow upon him this title. Their snarky faces drilled into us that boys who cried were not boys. They were, in fact, girls trapped in boys' bodies. So, he got the name stuck to his presence like the stale smell of smoke in a burnt house, inheriting it from one grade to another as we studied with the same kids. And because I look exactly like him – the same protruding nose, the same round eyes, the same wavy sweep of hair, the same light brown skin – I also inherited it.

The only good thing about school is that we can save up from the canteen money our father gives us and buy video games from the dingy mall facing our cadet college coaching at the end of every two weeks.

Today, Sohel got into a fight with Ishmam, a guy who ranks fifth in the hierarchy of the bullies. Ishmam stuck a pink gum on his collar during social studies class. Sohel did not notice it until I saw the gum hugging the sky blue fabric and pointed it out. Ishmam was sitting on the bench right behind Sohel. He snorted and laughed as I stared at him.

We were terrified; Sohel more than me. Because we knew how our father would react when he found the ugly remnants of gum on his collar. One time, my black shoes got scratches and thick marks of mud because of the rush at the canteen. That evening, after coming home from office, he did not even freshen up and started hitting my arms with his shoes. Their flat, hard edges jolted the nerves around my elbows and bruised my skin. I should have been careful and hidden them from the rack outside the door. Or I should have done the hard work of polishing them.

During the tiffin period, Sohel confronted Ishmam.

'Why did you do this?'

Ishmam was exchanging Pokémon cards with his friends on the last bench of the middle row.

'Ey, *hijra*. So what? What are you going to do?' he replied, his left arm resting on another boy's shoulder.

'He is going to hit you!' a boy from the group said while opening a packet of Mr. Twist.

And suddenly the air in the classroom turned smoky with anticipation as others, pushing benches, pushing one another, gathered and hoped for a spectacle.

'Oh really? Is this *hijra* going to hit me?'

Everyone laughed. Their shrill tones transformed into a resounding WOAAAH when Sohel actually hit him – a slap on his right cheek.

Ishmam, his hand covering his reddened cheek, stared at him in disbelief for a few seconds. And then he launched into thrashing him. Sohel fell across the desk behind. His sleeves ripped as Ishmam picked him up to slap him a few more times. His navy-blue pants turned yellowish brown from all the kicks. I urged my tears not to fall since that would mean more fodder for mockery – one brother crying for another. This was the first time one of us played a voluntary role in initiating a fight. Other times, it was just us being the victims of random assault and harassment in tiffin periods and after school breaks.

Sami, the class captain, arrived soon and stopped Ishmam, who resembled a steaming bull. Sohel got up, dusted his pants, and pulled up his bench and bag from the floor. His eyes were red and coated with tears. He put his face on the maroon bag and wrapped his arms around his head, shunning himself from the world.

*

Maghrib azan blares from the mosque across the street and swims in the evening air. Bats, crows, and kites fly home, crisscrossing the dim blue sky. We are waiting for the car, the smell of corn, kebab, smoke and piss snaking up our noses. In front of us, students are buying *jhaalmuri* and *fuchka* from the vendors lining up the streets, in spaces between parked cars and bikes.

The math test, as expected, did not go well because we were busy playing *Sims 3 and Assassins Creed: Revelations* the day before exam. Moreover, the fighting episode at the school today did not bode well for our non-existent enthusiasm.

Sohel suggests we change our father's phone number from the coaching centre's register book so that it cannot text the results to him anymore. A small white band-aid looks at me from the side of his forehead. He says we should walk up to the office room and tell the manager to edit his registry because our father 'has lost his previous phone'. I imagine he is being bold since the classroom incident enclosed him with a sense that one must stand up for oneself.

'Okay, but you will do it,' I reply.

Thankfully, the manager is too busy on his phone to quiz us about the change. We assume he is speaking to his wife. He is smiling, a halo of shyness borders his edges.

'Na, I will bring dinner. You do not have to cook.'

'Okay and how about Sylhet? That place is much better than Barisal.'

'Yeah, I will have to ask boss to give me three days of leave.'

We capture bits and scraps of his conversation.

We think he is not even listening to Sohel when he says that we need to change the number. He simply opens the registry book and hands over the green ballpoint pen to Sohel. He strikes across the number written and writes a new, fake one. We hurry out of the office, sliding shut the glass door behind. A soft lump of relief uncoils inside us, jumping up and down.

*

When it is Thursday – that dreaded weekly result day – father asks us why he still has not received a text from the centre. We say that the teacher notified us about how their services are temporarily down. He does not mind and fuss over this like we expect him to. He flutters his newspaper and dives inside. A cricket commentary spills from the radio. The driver curses at the rickshaw pullers drawing close to the car, which has, just today, received a squeaky-clean wash. I look at the *Call of Duty: Black Ops* cover on my lap. Sohel tugs at a thin strand of my hair to pass the disc packaging over to him. We are happy that we can go home, turn on the computer, insert the discs, install the game and play it without any heat on our cheeks, any stinging redness on our skins.

Now that we do not receive texts about our results, we wonder how much we are actually scoring. It has been more than two weeks. The shadows of tension that waited to fall over our house every Thursday are gone. The fact that so much time has passed by without getting hit by father is a welcome change – although we wish he would stop asking us how we did in our tests. Our nerves crawl in annoyance whenever he does it. That question always glazes his eyes with a kind of optimism that feels loaded with mockery – because the usual pattern is we suck at those tests and the optimistic glaze of his eyes melts and turns hellish. In our five daily Salahs, we pray to Allah that the present violence-free condition becomes a permanent resident of our house.

We turn on LifeOk at 10 p.m. to watch *Savdhaan India* while having dinner. Sohel glares at me and I realize the *daal* is about to fall off my plate on the white sofa. I immediately tilt the plate in the proper position. One time, at our grandmother's place, I committed the crime of spilling *daal* on the mosaic floor. He was, as you would expect, enraged. He trembled, bit his lower lip hard, clenched his fists and ran towards me from the living room. Our uncles, aunts and cousins froze as he pulled and twisted my ear before giving a final push on my shoulder that sent me flying towards the washroom door.

Tonight, the *Savdhaan India* case is about a man in Mumbai. He thinks that if his wife and daughters step out of the flat, they would be chased and assaulted by men in horrific ways. To prevent such a possibility, he decides to lock them up in the flat for seven years. They continue living in bestial conditions – starving and withering – while the neighbours do not get a whiff. He beats them when they protest or make attempts to get out. One fateful midnight, one of the daughters manages to escape and wanders for help on the streets. But he eventually catches up, drags her home through the empty, topaz streets, and what happens next is obvious – manic beating and extra layers of imprisonment measures. The scenes where the women cross their hands over their heads to dodge his fists and rods remind us of father doing the same with us (replace rods with plastic hangers in this case) although we are pretty sure he will never go as far as locking us up and torturing us for seven years. We eye each other for a moment, almost like there is a telepathic connection buzzing between me and Sohel. We do not say our thoughts out loud.

We blame our father for behaving roughly with us, but part of the blame goes to his mother.

Omar, our cousin, specifically our chacha's son who's three years older than us, told us a few months back why our father had turned out like that.

Chacha, chachi and Omar were in Bangladesh for Christmas holidays in England. We went to their place in Gulshan for a small dinner party that chachi hosted for us. She had hired a cook from Westin, although it was a gathering of immediate family members only – fuppi, her husband, their three daughters, me, Sohel and father.

We, the cousins, were in Omar's room, bored after playing monopoly and truth or dare for three hours straight. Omar noticed a red mark on my arm as I pushed my sleeve up to scratch the area. He patted my shoulder and motioned me to go to the balcony. I followed him.

'Your father is still beating you?' he asked.

Until then, I completely forgot that I had, in a moment of weakness, told him about our father's violence when he had visited Bangladesh last year.

I felt shy to reveal the truth. I nodded yes.

'I think I know why he's like this.'

'Why?'

'You see... don't tell anyone that you know this or that I told you this because my mother would kill me then.'

'I won't.'

'You promise?'

'I promise!'

'His mother stopped speaking to him for months after he got expelled from his cadet college for cheating on three tests consecutively in the tenth grade.'

I was silent. The coldness of the tiled floor seemed to climb up my legs.

'And then she died. Didn't even forgive him.'

'My father was in a cadet college?'

'You heard nothing from me. Absolutely nothing!'

I swatted at the mosquitoes buzzing around my arms.

'I think he just wants to fix his past through you two,' he added.

My heart was swollen. Not with a sense of sympathy for my father. But with anger at that woman for ruining our lives.

*

Ayon, one of our friends from the coaching, has a loving father. Unlike our father's greying beard, his is black and extends up to his chest. His bald head and his Lt. Colonel status in the army lend him an aura of harshness. We asked Ayon what his father did the time he had scored six out of twenty in the science test. Nothing, he said, carefully biting on an Oreo. We were flustered. In our imagination, his father had been stricter than ours, like *punching-him-after-tying-him-to-a-chair-with-ropes-in-a-dark-room-save-the-white-bulb-dangling-above* strict.

His car – a tea-brown Pajero from Bangladesh Border Guard – always arrives before ours. On the days his father comes, our hearts sink watching him greet Ayon with a wide, boyish smile, stroke his back, caress his curly hair, and take Ayon's bag from his sagging shoulders, carrying it all the way to the car.

A week ago, as we were waiting beside the *jhaalmuri* stall for our car following Ayon's departure, I asked Sohel: 'Should we ask father if he loves us?' He released a laughter tinged with hacking cough, a tiny burst of *jhaalmuri* falling from his mouth. 'What? No. Hell no. So childish.'

'I think he might,' I say.

'What makes you think so?'

I tell him what Omar told me, violating my promise.

'Now, see, he only mistreats us because he wants the best for us,' I add.

'Cut the nonsense,' he replies. He turns red and silent. His fists clench and unclench.

*

We bought *Need for Speed: The Run* today on our way home from the coaching. We were eyeing it for a month and anticipating that it might not run well on our computer. It took two hours to install. And it did run well, after we lowered the resolution two levels. We did not change out of our clothes. We kept on hammering away at our keyboard to steer our cars through rusty corn fields, rugged slopes and rain-coated roads. We did not notice how quickly time flew by and the call for Isha prayer snuck into our room through the open window beside Sohel's bed. As mosquitoes swam above our heads and sang around our ears, we realized we forgot to lock the windows after getting home. When father comes and finds all the mosquitoes, surely, he will take us to task. I get out of the chair and sprint towards my table. I pick up the aerosol bottle and spray the entire house with it so that he does not suspect our carelessness.

Just when I am about to sit beside Sohel and watch him speed against Lamborghinis, Audis and Porsches, my limbs exhausted from spraying all over, the telephone from the living room rings. I get up and answer the call, the telephone handle cold and wet against my palm because of the aerosol in the air.

'You devil!'

It is him, traffic sounds blaring in the background.

'You two lied to me?'

I cannot say anything. I feel like my stomach has absorbed all my words.

'I called the coaching centre today and Hannan told me you boys changed the number weeks ago. Just wait and see what I do after I reach home. Just wait, you wretched dogs!'

He cuts the call. I gulp. That dark *Savdhaan India* episode about the psycho father rises from the ground and floats before me, rousing shivers on my arms.

After I tell Sohel about this unwanted development, he screams. Then he prances around the room, jumps on the bed, pulls at his hair and curls into a ball under the computer table. The game is paused, the car waiting to be driven. I want to jump into the screen and be transported to that universe and speed into the sequoia-lined horizon under the pinkish orange sky. A few moments later, Sohel stands up and suggests that we take the money we have saved up all these weeks to buy more video games and leave.

'Are you out of your mind? Where the hell do you want to go?'

'I don't know. Let's just... leave first.'

'Can't we go to Fuppi's place?'

'No. He will drag us out if we go there. She pales before him.'

I do not reply. I watch as he takes the money from his drawer, ties the shoelaces of his red sneakers and presses the elevator button. Still reluctant about what course he is venturing into, I follow him, anxiously rubbing my hair. My belly gurgles. I want to throw up.

The night is suffused with heat. It breathes down on us, wrenching sweat from our depths, as if to say that we have no option except to return home. And yet we are walking and walking. Past the overbridge in front of the dilapidated cinema hall. Past the bus stand where people have gathered like bees in a hive and men scream from buses, calling out to passengers.

We do not stop walking even when we are in front of the shopping mall that used to be a hospital five years ago. The convention centre with Shah Rukh Khan's sunglass-sporting photo on its wall. The primary school that was the centre of a nationwide controversy last year for the rape of a third grader. The rows of flashy restaurants flaunting Lebanese, Turkish and Chinese cuisines.

A cool breeze caresses us. Sheets of dust, cigarette butts, styrofoam cups, polythene bags and discarded chips packets slide across the ground and take brief flights. A lone coconut tree rustles, a bunch of copper-coloured leaves descending on us. Vehicles pick up speed, honking extra loud. A herd of street kids wearing torn and grimy shirts scream, 'Rain!' and sprint across the footpath, some carrying large, empty pizza boxes. The sky grumbles, the sound heavy against our ears. We look up and through the mesh of wires and cables see a streak of lavender thundering down somewhere in the distance. We run to the opposite side of the road, stopping a rickshaw, a pharmacy lorry and a motorbike to let us cross. We enter the eatery where men are drinking tea and raucously chatting, some shouting into their phones. Our mouths water witnessing the *samochas* and *shingaras* being dipped in and out of a large black pan of oil. Standing at the entrance, we keep staring at the road as people in rickshaws hurriedly wrap blue tarpaulin sheets over themselves, as the light drizzle modifies into a heavy shower. Then comes hail. Like pellets they crash on the eatery's tin roof, mimicking the sound of a thousand metallic boots. Pellets crash on the eatery's tin roof. They sound like the marching of a thousand metallic boots.

They remind us of guns. Civilians, soldiers, aliens and ominous drug cartel owners from *Call of Duty*, *Just Cause*, *Mafia*, *The Godfather*, *Mass Effect* and GTA being sprayed with bullets.

And when they remind us of father's slaps, we flinch, the *thak-thak-thak* enveloping our ears.

My Human

1971

Niranjan and I are walking through a Sal forest. The sunlight is pouring on the uneven, rocky earth through the canopy. Birdsongs and cricket calls fill our ears. There's no food in sight nor any place for resting. The last time I ate was a few hours ago. We stumbled across a dead cow with a golden bell on its neck. A bullet hole in its forehead greeted me. Its belly was already open, flies buzzing in and out. Jackals, I assumed. I quickly wound my way around it, picking at the bones, the rotten flesh, and licking the matted blood. Niranjan waited while I ate. I felt bad for him, but I don't think his stomach would take the smell of entrails very well. Then a pack of feral pariahs came and shooed me away.

1969

In human time, I was a year old when Niranjan discovered me. The evening prayer echoed out of the minaret and settled on the neighbourhood. Rickshaws trilled on the streets. Pariahs stretched and wiggled their tails. Vendors lit up their lanterns and people gathered around for plates of *fuchka* and packets of *jhaalmuri*.

I had just given birth to six squeaky puppies, all flaunting a white coat, pink fleshy spots near their ears and snouts, their eyes squinted shut like they were in deep meditation regarding whether they should open them or not. At midnight, when the streets were quiet – except the howling of other pariahs and foxes, the hooting of owls and the chirping of crickets – some heartless rogues decided to pour gallons of hot water on us as we lay asleep on a cool, dusty slab by the car repair shop. One of my hind legs and brisket were completely burnt, my babies did not stir an inch. I ran, panted, howled and whimpered all night in pain. The neighbourhood grew alive with agony as the other dogs joined me in unison. We must have shattered the neighbourhood's sleep that night. Exhausted, the pain still throbbing up and down my whole being, I slowed down in front of a hushed apartment block and fell with a thud near a scooter that humans liked to call 'Lambretta'. I struggled to get up so I could at least take shelter under the car – which looked like a curious human whose ears always kept standing up – just a few paws away from the scooter. I could not reach it and fainted right beside the scooter.

I counted myself lucky to have fainted there. Otherwise, perhaps Niranjan might not have discovered me at all. The next morning, I was in a clinic where a lady applied various kinds of cool ointment on the burnt patches of my skin before bandaging me up. I stayed there for a week or so until Niranjan took me to his apartment. Every day that week, Niranjan – as the lady called him – visited me and asked after my health: 'How's she doing? When can I take her home?'

I found a new lease of life ever since I entered his apartment although the grief of losing my puppies and the burning pain still rattled me. He named me Woolf, after one of his favourite writers, a lady from a faraway land. She was called Virginia Woolf. I did not like it at first, but then I heard him say to his friend one day in the living room how my howling almost resembled a wolf's – every pariah I knew had the same kind of howling by the way – and how naming me after one of his favourite figures 'just made perfect sense. Like two things falling into their designated positions without any obstacles'. And so, I embraced the name wholeheartedly. The fact that I had been named after one of his favourite people and therefore I could share the same pedestal as that Virginia Woolf lady blew softly over every pained nerve inside me.

Niranjan had short and neatly oiled hair that gleamed under the glowing light. He wore glasses with thick frames. His shirt was always ironed straight without any wrinkles, tucked inside his pants, enclosed by a spotless and shiny belt. I assumed he must have been one of those teachers I used to see on the road after the school had been emptied of its students.

Niranjan snored while he slept. One of his arms remained slung over me. He liked the furry warmth coating his skin. But I mostly did not. So, I wriggled myself free when I felt particularly annoyed with this habit. But on days I felt a strange surge of sympathy and love for him, I let his arm remain. Before sleeping, he wrote late into the night, the lantern burning bright beside his notepad on the desk, mosquitoes buzzing around his ears and legs. He muttered to himself while writing. Sometimes he even read his writing out loud in a pretentiously thick voice, walking in swift strides about the room, holding the paper in one hand before him while the other hand rested around his back. He often slid his fingers around his hair and pulled at the strands and shouted before tearing a paper and throwing it in a bin.

He sometimes cried while doing that. I assumed he must have been frustrated with his writing. So, I quickly jumped on his lap and snuggled there, his one hand softly stroking my back while the other wrote.

Niranjan was a history teacher at the St. Joseph English Medium School on Asad Avenue. He taught the sixth grade. He headed out for the school every morning at 7 when half of the sun still lay behind the clouds and the roosters from the ground floor did not abstain from screaming throatily. Before heading out, he prayed to the tiny idol of 'Durga', which remained perched inside a glittery box on his desk. He came back in the afternoon, sometimes with three or four male friends from the workplace and sometimes with one woman, whose name was Nilima. When he came with his male friends, they sat in the living room, chatted, laughed heartily, ate puffed rice and chips, drank lemonade and talked about politics. One time, Niranjan said: 'I really hope those Pakistanis from the central government withdraw the wretched Agartala Case and acquit Sheikh Mujibur Rahman'.

Hasib: 'I don't think they will. It's the BENGALIS' demand for some degree of autonomy, after all. See how it can bruise their conscience?'

Animesh: 'Look, whatever happens, at the end of the day, it's people like me and Niranjan who will be looked down upon by the Pakistanis because we are Hindus. We are Indian agents! So be careful while you folks hang out with us. We can kidnap you and take you to India and ask for secret information from the Pakistani government in exchange for your worthless lives.' Then the whole gang roared with laughter. And when he came with Nilima, the miasma of raspy voices tittering-shouting-lecturing was missing. Only the delightful combination of

Nilima and Niranjan's quiet chuckling remained. She usually stayed longer than the guys. They did not munch on puffed rice and chips. They cooked daal, chicken and rice together. I realized that the food was always better when she had a hand in cooking; the meat of the chicken perfectly slender, the bones not excessively coated with spices. After lunch, as Niranjan remained busy washing the dishes, Nilima clutched me in a hug and plunged her face into my neck. It tickled me and I squirmed all over her head, ruffling the smooth plait of her hair and licked her nose. Then we crashed on the sofa and Niranjan came over, rubbing his wet hands on the sides of his trousers. They talked and cuddled (with me beside them) until the 4.30 p.m. azan seeped into the apartment. I felt like a child protected by her loving parents. She always left during the 4.30 p.m. azan, after moving her hands up and down my back and kissing Niranjan's cheek. Whenever they talked, the topic was mostly centred around marriage.

Nilima: 'When do you think we should ask our parents to get us married?'

Niranjan: 'I honestly don't know. I want to marry you, I really do... but you know how they are. If they find our horoscope is conflicting, they will not approve of our marriage.'

Nilima: 'This fear shouldn't be stopping us from asking them, Jaan.'

Niranjan: 'I know, but—'

Nilima: 'Look, we have been seeing each other for almost two years now. We are teachers at the same school, we grew up together at the colony in Puran Dhaka, our mothers have been friends since their childhood, our families know one another too well... I don't think there's anything likely to stop us.'

1970

Nilima and Niranjan got married with zero astrological resistance. Had babies even. A pair of twin boys: Ashutosh and Anjum. I loved licking the twins' noses and cheeks. I particularly enjoyed digging my snout into their bouncy bellies, into the folds of their powdered necks. They reminded me of my puppies who were snatched from me too soon. I cried when nobody looked.

But Nilima... something was off about her ever since the babies had tumbled out of her. She often groaned and swatted my face away when I tried getting closer to the babies wriggling on the bed. Once, I heard her say to Niranjan, 'Jaan, I don't like it when Woolf comes near the babies. I don't hate her, but it's so risky! What if she bites her and they get rabies?' Niranjan grabbed her shoulders and laughed. 'You worry too much!' he said. A breeze of relief shrouded me because Niranjan hadn't changed his view of me despite Nilima's insistence.

She stopped spending time with me except when she gave me food. All her attention now revolved around the twins. I had no grudge about that. But... couldn't she show me some affection like before? I was not asking for much. Just a tiny fraction of the previous levels.

As I later learned when Niranjan and Nilima were engaged in a verbal warfare inside their room on my account (Nilima had insisted that evening I should be relocated somewhere else until the kids grew up), Nilima's friend and her baby had been bitten by their dog. It was surprising because she was, like me, a neutered animal. But how could I say to Nilima that I would never hurt Ashutosh and Anjum? I wanted to teach that dog a lesson for defiling the reputation of non-harmful canines like myself. I was disappointed at how Nilima's mind was so flaky regarding me. I didn't want to hold on to the disappointment, though, because I guessed mothers tended to be like that. Perhaps, if my pups hadn't been killed, I would have turned out like Nilima. Perhaps, I would have instructed my pups to not venture into Mohammadpur, to not be friends with the fancy foreign pups, who were snobbish because they lived in bungalows with the rich.

I did not like the Niranjan vs. Nilima episodes that soared every time she floated the topic of temporarily getting me out of the apartment. So, I went to the veranda and poked my head out of the banister's posts. I counted how many rickshaws and scooters passed by the road, how many crows returned home, how many tufts of clouds floated in the mauve sky. It helped me divert my attention from their fight.

Niranjan began staying out late after office. This led to an additional bitterness in their relationship. He would often come home drunk with an empty bottle of brandy, a loose tie and a ruffled shirt. Nilima wouldn't sleep with him on those nights. He cried himself to sleep, mumbling unintelligible words to me, on the couch. He was clear enough only one time.

'I am super tired, Woolf. Like, very... tired. I can't handle her requests. She makes me feel like I don't love my children. I do love them, goddamnit! I'm sorry, Woolf. I'm sorry she thinks badly of you,' he said, patting my forehead, before hugging me and drenching my neck with his tears.

One Monday, Nilima slapped him when he returned after 12 a.m. 'How dare you stay out this late?' she shouted. 'Who is she? Is she better than me?' she added. 'What? What the hell is wrong with you?' Niranjan replied, blinking, yawning and leaning on the door for balance. I thought this made Nilima angrier. *How dare he turn up in this inebriated state!* she must have thought. She scoffed and titled her head. She went inside the room and locked the door. Niranjan got one of his leather notebooks from under the TV and scribbled down words. This was the first time in a long time I saw him write. He had stopped that after Nilima's delivery. I couldn't read so I remained clueless. He cried and wrote, cried and wrote. He tore out the pages that had become wet with his tears falling on them. Then he fell asleep on my back.

After that incident, I barely saw them speak. He made his own breakfast. Sometimes, he made scrambled eggs for her. She refused to eat them and sufficed herself with apples and bananas. Sometimes, he chopped vegetables and cut chicken before going to the school for her ease. She threw them into the bin. I snooped inside the bin and ate the pieces of chicken even though Niranjan had banned raw chicken for me because I had a long spell of food poisoning after consuming raw chicken a long time ago.

He was now a regular sleeper in either the living room or the spare bedroom, depending on his mood, while Nilima slept with the babies.

When he proposed to Nilima that they go for a day out to Ramna Park, Nilima left the dining table. He followed her inside the room, and a fight ensued. I wasn't actively eavesdropping, but I could make out the words from the living room and the veranda:

'I promise I'll stop drinking, Jaan... No, for the love of god, I'm not seeing other women!'

1971

When I woke up, I wished I hadn't. In the dining room, Nilima and Niranjan bawled like children, clutching one another, leaned against the table, and a dishevelled man in a bloodied white shirt and lungi softly sobbed before them. They kept crying even after the man left. I felt a little ball of relief jumping in my heart seeing them close together after so long. Ashutosh and Anjum peeked into the living room from behind the florid curtains covering the bedroom's entrance.

I lay stretched on Niranjan and Nilima's laps. They still cried and smoothened the fur on my back, her head in his shoulder, his head above hers. It was surprising to feel Nilima's hand on my fur. Did she suddenly change? What did I miss? I kept wondering what they cried about.

Nilima turned her head away and said, 'Do you think Prakash was perhaps mistaken? Perhaps he saw some other bodies that looked like our parents'?' Thick snot forming around Niranjan's nose. He took off his glasses and rubbed his tears and snot with the cuff of his Panjabi and replied, 'No, Jaan. He practically saw them begging the bastards for mercy before they gunned them down.'

Inside me, something loosened. A terrible sense of sorrow connected me with my humans in a way I had never felt before. Finally, all of us had licked the hands of loss (me losing my puppies, them losing their parents), having to bid our loved ones goodbye without sensing that this specific moment was the last one we could share with them, and so we should hold them and touch them and kiss them and hug them and inhale the memory of their existence. In any case, the silver lining was that Nilima's grievance stemming from Niranjan's drinking seemed to not exist anymore. All that existed was grief.

Niranjan and Nilima threw everything they thought necessary – strips of medicines, bottles of cough syrup, bags of puffed rice and biscuits, a carton of juice, some of their clothes and the twins' dresses, some burkhas the Khans from the house downstairs had given them for safety, the miniature Durga tightly wrapped and hidden inside a fluffy towel – into the medium-weight metal trunk. We were joining the Devs that midnight. They had secured a man who could ferry us across the Buriganga, from where we would find some other men who would take us to India. Nilima placed all of her jewellery in a box which she kept in her handbag. Niranjan put his chains and watches – some imported from England via his uncle – into the leather bag he used to take to office. Their valuables were 'the price we had to pay for reaching into safety.'

The boatman had a *gamcha* wrapped around his head. He cautiously kept scanning the horizon as he rowed the boat, the water cackling with each hit of the oar. From time to time, he took the oar on his lap and pried free the tresses of water hyacinths. Inside the half-circular shed, us were boiling. We remained quiet, the Devs on one side, and we on another. The adults had to remain bent and ducked because the roof was so low. We could not light a lantern in case that alerted the army. Mosquitoes brought out welts on our skins. Ashutosh accidently poked my eye while looking for a biscuit from the small tin. Because it was dark and Nilima couldn't see, I licked his cheek. Couldn't reach for Anjum's, though, because he was on Nilima's lap.

Soon, a barrage of bullets hit the boat. The boatman plopped into the water. Everyone inside the shed tried their best to lie down and avoid them. I felt suffocated. Who was on top of me? Perhaps the neighbour's wife? Or wait... the minty breath... is it Anjum? I felt liquid trickling into my fur, coating the burnt patch of my hind legs. Then came some more bullets, some more liquid trickling into my coat over the brisket, the ears, the neck. Oh wait... a moan, a terrible moan... a cry, a child crying, a man, a woman... who is it? No, please, don't die. We have to reach India, remember? No, no, no, please don't die anyone!

A few minutes after the bullets let up, I heard Niranjan cry and gasp for breath. A repulsive stench was torturing my nostrils. I wriggled myself free from the bodies above me and jumped at Niranjan, whose face was smeared with blood. I realized everyone except us had been hit. The only bodies that moaned now were Dev's and Ashutosh's. The others were motionless. Niranjan quivered as he grabbed Ashutosh, his throat spilling blood. 'Don't go, please, don't go, don't don't, don't.'

All night, he cried, with no care about the possibility of being captured by the army. I wept, too, recalling all those moments I had shared with Nilima and the twins. I sniffed her body. Then the twins' bodies. Ohh, the awful smell of death! Niranjan's eyes turned red. They reminded me of the homeless man who inhaled white powder at night and shooed me away whenever I came near him in Farmgate. I hugged him as his body rose and fell like he was having trouble breathing. I crawled towards Nilima, wiped her face with my paws and rubbed her face with my snout. 'Oh, Jaan, please forgive me!' he let out. 'I am sorry for turning into a drunkard. I am sorry for not listening to you. Please come back. I promise I will send Woolf away and stop drinking. I promise we will have no fights after that. Please come back!' His ranting grew faint, and he fell asleep beside Nilima. The smell of blood waved in the night. So did a sense of discomfort and deception.

*

I miss Nilima and the twins. How wonderful it would have been had we not been discovered by the military. Perhaps we would be in India by this time, away from the stronghold of death, but we are not. We are in a forest. Niranjan and me. Walking nowhere in particular.

I wish dogs had a way of conveying to their humans that we understand whatever you say to others. If that were the case, I would be able to convey how betrayed I felt by his words: 'I promise I will send Woolf away...' I wanted to separate myself from him for a brief period of time. His eyes, his lips, his hair, everything screamed betrayal. But I know I cannot be a disloyal dog. I cannot be ungrateful to the man who rescued me.

Moreover, the last time Niranjan ate was two days ago. I need to be around him to make sure he gets to eat something.

We were with a group that also had been misplaced from their route due to the military's indiscriminate firing. During the day, we rested in the forests. At night, we walked, a hush shrouding us, on a road that promised to lead us towards India.

We hid in the bushes and thickets whenever a jeep or a truck approached. One time, a baby started crying as we lay hidden while four soldiers chatted among themselves in Urdu, a language I had heard people – mostly people from Mohammadpur – speak but could not understand myself. They discovered the baby and its mother, dragged them out of the bush and stomped it to death while the mother wailed and begged. They pushed her into the jeep and drove away. Luckily, there were no other people hiding around the mother and her baby. After the jeep had driven away, we came out of hiding and started walking, some of us consoling the man who had just lost his wife and child. He did not look even once at the baby lying dead on the road. He was stiff.

The next morning, as we gathered in a circle for breakfast (biscuits, chips and bottles of juice everyone had scoured from an abandoned lorry nearby), a boy from our group ran towards us and shouted, pointing his finger to the direction where the

Bodhi tree stood. He was unable to utter words. When we went there, we found the man lying at the base of the tree, his skull torn open, streaks of blood splattered on the bark. Everyone winced and muttered prayers under their breaths for the man who had killed himself.

In the afternoon, the military raided the forest. We dispersed. Many ran away unscathed; some fell down as bullets stormed upon us like an empire of insects. We never saw the survivors again.

Only the dead lay scattered around us. Niranjan and I hid in a small waterhole. After the soldiers left, we got out of our hiding spot, and Niranjan scoured our now-destroyed makeshift resting area for food items. Not much food was left; a few packets of chips that only lasted for two days. Poor Niranjan. At that moment, I wished he could eat things off the street like my kind does.

In any case, we are not in India, and Niranjan is exhausted from hunger. He eats berries from the bushes and trees, but they're not helping him gain energy. When we were with the group, we came upon jackfruit trees bearing ripe jackfruits. We plucked and dove into them to our relief. Now they don't seem to be anywhere near us. Niranjan slows down and sits against a tree. His eyes are closed, he moans, and says, 'Oh God... oh God', his hands tightly holding his stomach. I panic and start roaming around him, panting and wiggling my tail. He can't die. I fetch a few berries and leaves from the thicket beside him and he gobbles them up, then chokes, swallows some of them, and spits the rest out. Beads of sweat trickle off the bridge of his nose.

'Woolf,' he says and carries me to his lap. His sweaty face rests on my back. 'You're a good dog, Woolf,' he says, his voice drawls, sounding like when he and his friends would get drunk at the apartment. 'You've always been a good dog,

Woolf.' His face keeps rubbing my back. I don't like it, but I am broken seeing Niranjan in this state. 'If there's a heaven for dogs, I hope you go there. Good dog. Good Woolf.' He drifts into sleep. He no longer snores. I clamber out of his clutch, and he falls on the ground. I curl up over his belly, the words still vibrating my ears: 'I promise I will send Woolf away.'

Not long after, I see a group of seven Pakistani soldiers in Khaki unforms, olive hats, and black boots emerge from behind the clump of Arecanut trees. They are dragging three blindfolded men through the ground with ropes. One of the soldiers throws a glance in our direction. This is it, I think. Niranjan will turn into one of those men. I will try to protect him, like I tried protecting my pups all those years ago and end up dead as well. He must think Niranjan is dead and I am a random dog because he turns his face away and heads forward with the group. They disappear into a narrow opening in the thickets ahead. Relief whooshes inside my chest. I lick Niranjan's face. It's coated in a salty musk because the rays won't stop spilling through the canopy.

Behind me, a screech. Then another. Two squirrels gut a green bud in turns. I leap and chase them. One escapes with a slight scratch of my claws on its back. Another struggles to breathe beneath my paws. Its eyes roll, tail flutters. As I bare my teeth and lower my head, I think of Niranjan. He must eat it no matter what. He cannot survive on stems and leaves for long. That diet makes him retch. I wish dogs had the ability to be persistent – like parents – with their humans. Then I could put food in his mouth forcibly. Like Nilima did with the twins when they would shake their heads as a spoonful of yellow porridge floated in front of their faces.

I cannot let him die even though his words still roil in my ears.

Bilal

Bilal was born blind in the left eye. It was as if he owned a marble for an eye. But the saving grace was that he was not a dark boy like most of us; if you placed him beside a cow's udder, you would think they were spun out of the same soil but moulded in different forms. We bullied him, shouting, 'here comes the white ghost!' when he entered the class or joined us in the afternoons by the lake.

Initially, Bilal did not cry because of our relentless bullying. It was in the third grade when we first spotted him crying under the mango tree beside the rusty school gate. After the discovery, we started calling him a girl. From girl, it morphed into *hijra*, as suggested by Arif, the shortest boy in our group. Perhaps Bilal should not have let us discover him crying, since that only lent us more energy in bullying him. Ever since, Bilal grew more accustomed to crying. Not in secret. Right in front of us, tears crowding his eyes, spilling down his cheeks like rainwater trickling down the mildewed walls in our classroom.

The fact that he never fought back when we, without reason, pushed him, poked him in the chest, slapped his cheeks, pulled his ears, tousled his neat, oiled hair and rumpled his already-wrinkly shirt, wrenching it out of his loose, worn-out belt's grip only emboldened us. It gave our calling him *hijra* unending validity.

Once, he could not answer when the teacher asked the result of twelve multiplied by seven, and the teacher hit both his palms with the thick yellow ruler always poking out of his brown pocket like an extra limb straining to grow out of him. As we expected, Bilal began crying. When we bully him, he cries, sure, but in whimpers. However, after receiving the *thwack-thwacks*, he did. From the next day, the teacher started calling him a 'good girl British girl' and 'my darling Bilkis', pushing the whole class into a long bout of laughter. From then, we used these words to shout at Bilal.

Neither our teachers nor our mothers (except Hamid's mother, who, like Hamid, adored Bilal) could stand him.

He could not do simple multiplications and divisions and narrowly escaped failing the third grade. We could pluck the teachers' disdain for him from the way their eyes rolled, their nostrils flared, the long sighs they exhaled or the stern voices they wore while calling Bilal for giving him his poorly marked exam copy or asking him to solve a math problem or write the meaning of a tough Bangla word.

'Don't be like Bilal,' our Bangla teacher said, her face surprisingly calm and composed, after handing out the midterm copies. He had scored nine out of hundred, the lowest in our class. We were sure that Bilal had received his fair share of punishment from her. When we were playing tag the next day, we noticed that his palms were purple.

For reasons we did not know, our mothers called him 'the fruit of evil'. They told us to stay away from him, although not strictly, only when they saw us with him. So, we thought it would not be the end of the world to have him around. Their negative view of him was like a ghost on our shoulders that repeatedly assured us that it was okay to act rough with him.

Our mothers did not get along with Bilal's mother as well. They shot a glance towards her and muttered things under their breath whenever they accidentally crossed paths in the fields, the markets, or the monthly village fairs. From our group, Sohail's mother was the staunchest hater of Bilal and his mother.

Whenever our mothers backbit about them, hers was the loudest and most passionate voice. Hamid's mother always condemned the backbiting sessions and, accordingly, left in fury when one was taking place. Quoting the Holy Qur'an, she said that backbiters are among the topmost sufferers in hell. 'All of you will be eating the flesh of your own siblings in the hereafter, you know that?!'

One summer, after school, Bilal accidentally poked Sohail's eye while stretching his hands as he yawned. We were huddled under the mahua tree, sipping ice-cola and lemonade, our school bags lying scattered around the bunioned roots. Sohail wanted to beat Bilal up very badly but could not muster the strength with the pain in his eye. That evening, his mother stormed into the tiny shack Bilal and his mother lived in, drew Bilal out and gave him a decent amount of lashes having picked up a birch twig from the ground. Before delivering the last blow, the left sleeve of her blouse tore open slightly at the shoulder. 'You fatherless devil! How dare you hit my son?' she shouted, her eyes bloodshot and glaring, tears glistening on her face. We had never seen Sohail's mother so enraged before. We were confused at her rage. After all, wasn't it something that Sohail himself should have dealt with the next day, before or after school? Would our mothers have reacted the same way if he accidentally hit us someday? We wondered.

People from the neighbouring shacks and houses also gathered to observe the spectacle, some came with lanterns, cutting the dusky gloom. Bilal's mother helplessly whimpered, leaning against a wooden pool in front of the door, as Bilal lay dusty and crying on the bare earth. The sound of crows returning home mingled with his sobs. After Sohail's mother left, Bilal's mother hurried towards him and locked him in a tight embrace. Then they cried together, reminding us of the dogs in the paddy fields crying their last cries after receiving snake bites.

Every afternoon we played cricket or football after school, and Bilal quietly sat at the base of the coconut tree and watched birds, sometimes squinting his eyes when the sun was too bright, sometimes running across the field, crashing against cows and goats, sticking his feet into dung, to catch a better glimpse of the flocks shooting farther and farther away. He joined us when we played tag or hide and seek. Only Hamid gave him brief company during breaks while playing cricket or football. We were sure Hamid was bored by the talk of birds Bilal started then, but he could not – would not – express his true emotion in front of Bilal.

We could not shout insults at Bilal when Hamid was around him. We loved Hamid. He was the boy who came first in our class. He was the best batsman among us. He was the kind of boy who always had a halo of kindness floating about him, who always reminded you of God. We believed in Him, but we did not pray five times a day like Hamid did.

Hamid had an elevated position in our eyes, no doubt. He often lectured us about Allah's wrath on those who cruelly treated another human being, especially during the times we hurt Bilal. Like when Shafi tied a chewing gum in Bilal's hair and a circular patch from his crown had to be cut off; Bilal had to wear a skullcap to school every day for two weeks.

But did this stop us from bullying Bilal?

No.

After all, who was 'the fruit of evil'?

Bilal was.

Who had a ghostly eye and ghostly skin?

Bilal did.

Who made the teachers scrunch up their faces and want to pull his sideburns *upupup*?

Bilal did.

Were not all these signs from God that Bilal was a despicable vessel?

Yes, of course.

*

The final examination questions were tougher than wood apple skin. Especially English, science and math. We had to study late into the nightly hours because the math teacher had warned us, in his usual, annoying nasal voice, 'Your questions will be tough. So, prepare accordingly. Be mindful of your class notes, understand? Especially you, my darling Bilkis.' In the evenings, we thronged in Hamid's house and gobbled up the spicy puffed rice his mother served as he explained the class lectures. We reduced our afternoon playing hours and studied in the field together, the goats' sporadic bleating seeping into our memory as we memorized poems. Math problems and science questions rattled in our heads. We grew lax when it came to being our usual selves with Bilal since so much studying was dampening our energy.

The whole class managed to pass the third grade. Except Bilal. It did not rain down on us as something unexpected. Our initial thought was to tease him about the matter. But then we learned that his mother had withdrawn him from the school after the results came in. She could not afford to pay for an extra year. The peon told us she had begged the teachers and cried before them for mercy so that they would allow Bilal to pass. But they did not. Instead, some of them – the math and the social science teacher, he remembered – asked her for a heavy sum! Bribe! It escaped us how our teachers, who spoke highly of virtue and good manners, could ask for bribe. Hamid strode around the room, calming himself, before telling us how these teachers, these bribe takers, would be residents of hell.

In any case, Bilal was gone from the school. He now joined his mother as an extra helper at the house where she worked as a maid.

The house belonged to the Jamils, the richest family in the village. They owned most of the lands here. It was because of them that the school had a roof at least, although not a very good one when it came to holding back heavy rain. It was because of them that there were wells scattered across the village, which made it possible for the villagers to fetch water easily instead of travelling miles for the purpose.

We did not have anyone from that family in our group. Their only child, Saif, was older than us. He had gone off to the capital as an engineering student but returned after two years without finishing his university education and had become a drunkard. He mixed with the goon types. The useless fellows who teased and harassed girls to marry them and shopkeepers to give them free items. He looked intimidating anyway with his bushy beard, raspy voice and muscular body. And the drinking made him even more intimidating. He became acerbic in his speech and movement like a machine whose battery would never get exhausted. His father, Musa, was a clever man. He used Saif as well as the men who guarded his property to threaten farmers who did not pay taxes in due time for farming on his land.

Bilal's absence in the fourth grade made us realize how much we missed him. We missed his wrong answers, his dozing off in class, his crying after the beating sessions, his quiet, frowned-upon existence on the last bench. He scarcely joined us in the afternoons now, only once every week and sometimes not even then. When we asked why he remained missing lately, he said he had too much work to do at the Jamils.

We did not bully him anymore.

One reason was that Bilal seemed more shrunken now than before. He became pale. Dark half-moons appeared under his eyes. His hair lost its lustre and grew stiff. He reeked of soap and fish. He wore torn and grubby shirts.

Another – perhaps the main – reason was that Hamid, whose virtue achieved an authoritative force after we entered the fourth grade, threatened us he would leave our group if we bullied Bilal ever again in any manner.

We noticed a purple bruise on Bilal's forehead when he came to play tag with us after a whole month. We asked him how he got injured now that there were no teachers to beat him up or no bullying from our group either. He replied that Musa had hit him with a vase because he thought Bilal had stolen his blue kurta, which was soon found beneath a heap of just-washed clothes waiting to be hung on the clothesline. Hamid seethed, clenching his fists.

The next week, there was a brown, crusty patch on his knee. Reason: Musa's wife, Zainab, spotted a yellow stain on her new *shari* which she had given to Bilal for washing and shoved him so hard he fell down the stairs.

Two weeks after that, long red scratch marks lined his arms. Reason: Zainab ran a fork down his arms because he had mistakenly thrown away a fork in the garbage bin.

New bruises appeared on him every time he joined us: a cut on his cheek, a swelling on his eyebrow, a dark line on his lower lip, a red ridge slanted across his neck. This happened so many times that we stopped enquiring after a while. We felt sorry for him thinking that school was a less cruel place compared to the Jamils' place.

We also felt guilty for bullying him so much in the past. Now we brought him chips, lemonade and ice-colas whenever he hung around with us.

Sometimes we saw him on the field beside the mosque. His hand tied to the rope tugging at the Jamils' smallest cow as he watched birds zapping across the sky. Sometimes we saw him at the market, fetching groceries and hauling large sacks that seemed capable of breaking his bones. Even our mothers – except Sohail's – grew kind towards him after we told them of Bilal's ordeal. We saw some of them helping Bilal haul the bags one time. Another time, they sent steaming rice and mutton to Bilal's shack.

No matter how much the women convinced her, Sohail's mother refused to budge. 'Areh, let go of your bitterness, *bhabi*. Can't you see how much the poor soul is suffering?' one of our mothers said. To which, Sohail's mother replied, 'But my husband isn't coming back, is he?' We did not understand how the death of Sohail's father was related to the subject of Bilal.

The next day, as we lazily walked home after school, the sun baking us mercilessly, we asked Sohail what his mother meant. Sohail said he did not know either. He said he would ask her once he reached home. That afternoon, while setting up the cricket stamps using bricks from the construction site beside the field, Sohail came running towards us. His mother had answered him.

Sohail's father was killed by the Pakistani military when he joined the war in 1971. The same military that had captured Bilal's mother during the war. She was pregnant when they released her and later gave birth to Bilal. So, it turned out Bilal did not have a father because he was languishing somewhere in Pakistan.

Now we understood why our mothers used to call him 'the fruit of evil', why the teachers could not stand him (the teachers could not stand dumb students anyway, but their attitude towards him was particularly colder than it was towards other dumb students).

We groaned, exasperated at what he told us. Tears clumped around his eyelids. He wanted to kill Bilal for being 'a Pakistani Satan'.

Hamid sat up, wiping the grass stains from his pants, and shouted at Sohail. 'How is it his fault?'

Sohail, teary-eyed and fuming, lunged at Hamid. He fell to the ground, and we intervened, holding Sohail back as if he were a mad bull.

He wanted to break free and beat Hamid to a pulp. Hamid stared back, enraged, his jaws throbbing like a big man's. He did not lunge back. He simply closed his eyes and took deep breaths to calm himself before leaving the field.

After that incident, an uneasiness settled in our group and cleaved it in two. Some of us took Hamid's side, choosing to continue to be kind to Bilal, and some of us took Sohail's, choosing to throw stones at him whenever he could be spotted. Now we did everything separately: playing, hanging around, sitting in the classroom. Cricket, football, hide-and-seek and tag were not as fun anymore. We missed the original gang. Some of us had kernels of hope that the group would automatically repair soon.

But one day, at Kazi Chacha's tea stall, Sohail told Saif about Bilal's history and asked him if it would be possible to torture him more than his family already did. Saif let out a snort-mixed laughter and nodded in agreement.

This led to a war between Team Hamid and Team Sohail.

Before the war began, both teams assumed soldier-like mannerisms, wielding cricket bats, twigs and bamboo sticks. It was especially shocking to see Hamid gearing up for battle. His calm and focused eyes oozed determination as he rubbed his hands across the brown bamboo stick. Perhaps, he should not have forgotten that Team Hamid was much smaller than Team Sohail, and so defeat was a highly practical possibility. As expected, Team Hamid gave up five or six minutes into the war as noses bled, knees bruised, teeth broke and shirts tore from both parties. Only Hamid kept wrestling with Sohail as the rest stood watching, not intervening. Only when Sohail shouted for help did the boys from his side separate them from the seemingly fatal bearhug. Hamid had a patch of Sohail's hair in his hand. Sohail's sideburn bled, his blue shirt flaunting the drops. Sohail shouted at his team to charge against Hamid, but everyone felt it too cruel to launch an attack on Hamid, since he was now alone without his team.

Like Sohail wanted, Bilal received more torture from the Jamils than before. When we spotted him at the market or at the field, we almost failed to recognize him. One day, there was an oval-shaped burn on his cheek, which first appeared to us like a mole. Another day, we saw half of his left arm bandaged and another half coated with some yellow ointment over the almost-bare flesh. The Jamils' cruelty angered us. All members of Team Sohail, save three, switched over to Team Hamid. The hope of reunification now suffused the air. The returnees said that Sohail had increasingly become too obsessed with torturing Bilal, that he often met up with Saif and drank the alcohol from his maroon bottle as he told Sohail all the things they did with Bilal. We did not want to know what they did.

The sky opened when we were one goal away from breaking the tie. Goats whined and ran to take cover under trees. We jumped, took off our shirts, screamed and ran towards no direction in particular, the earth, hot and wet, sucking at our dusty feet.

At one point, thanks to Arif, we realized that we were before the Jamils' gate. We looked at one another and decided to peep inside through the hole at the centre. We were not tall enough to reach it, so we decided to climb on each other's back so that one of us – Hamid, we decided – could take a look. He said he could not see much. Only the big black cows chewing hay under the shed; Bilal's mother picking up the fallen mangoes; the chickens thrashing in the coop, annoyed at the rain; Saif smoking a beedi on the porch, playing cards with his friends. We loitered around for a while and frequently peeped inside hoping to catch a glimpse of Bilal until the guards spotted us and chased us away, shouting 'Come here, you little thieves. Will give you such a beating you will forget how to steal mangoes!'

That reminded us we could have easily stolen mangoes from the tree outside the gate.

Our mothers shunned Sohail's from their gang on account of his turning a drunkard at such a young age. They were glad to know that we did not mix with Sohail anymore. Even the three remaining members of his team left and joined us. Sohail was sighted with Saif and his thug friends all the time now. Even though he was made a slave to their lowly antics, like fetching their alcohol bottles and beedis, arranging their cards, distributing warnings to the farmers yet to pay taxes, he put on a haughty smirk when we crossed paths. We hated his smirk. It seemed as if Sohail put on the smirk to show us that he now moved around with influential hooligans.

Hamid and his mother visited their shack late one night when Bilal was home with his mother. Hamid told us how Bilal did not speak much, how he had shrunken even more into himself, how his bruises expanded – the largest one was on his back. He told him it was Sohail who scalded that area with a hot ladle when Saif and his friends, drunk, had locked him in their room for fun and asked Sohail to do 'something inventive' to Bilal. Hearing him, we realized we were powerless. All we could do was feel sadness swimming into our hearts. Perhaps that made us kind enough in the eyes of Allah. But Hamid wanted to do something meaningful. He wanted to liberate Bilal from the Jamils' clutches. We told him how foolish it was to pursue something futile. He groaned and stomped on a tiny clump of touch-me-not plants outside the school gate.

What happened the next week shook us all. It was something that would haunt the village for a lifetime.

'Death to Pakistan!' they chanted before launching their sticks on Bilal's torso. Bilal was tied with a rope to the rain tree in front of the Jamils' house. Two white arcs replaced his eyebrows. We had to look hard to make sure it was Bilal. Where were his eyebrows? A huge crowd thronged on the field to witness the violence at the hands of the guards unfold.

Bilal's mother screamed and fell at the men's legs, but they kept kicking her away. When she did not stop, two of the men pinned her to the ground as she kept screaming for Bilal and wriggling like an animal before sacrifice.

Saif was standing behind the beaters, his hands blended into a lock across his chest, his gaze fixed on Bilal. Among them, we could not notice Sohail, whose presence there we would not have found surprising. We could not understand why exactly Bilal was being beaten. We assumed he must have been wrongly accused of stealing or damaging something expensive in the house. Some winced at the piercing cries Bilal let out after each hit, some had tears spilling out of their eyes, some watched determinedly, some mournfully, some shouted 'Death to Pakistan!' in unison. When Hamid reached the venue, he screamed like the muscles of his face would soon tear apart. Still screaming, he charged towards the guards. One blow on his neck, and he fell on the hot earth, unconscious.

When he woke up at his house, we told him that Bilal had been killed.

*

The August heat wrung our throats dry. Our bottles were empty, our school bags heavy on our shoulders. There was no stall around us, only shrubs and green paddy fields. We looked up at the ashen sky dotted with kites flying so high they looked like mosquitoes and prayed for it to split open. As we proceeded home, we saw Sohail running towards us. We had not sighted him anywhere since Bilal's death, which was nearly two months ago. Everyone at the school thought he had dropped out and moved out of the village. He broke down and fell on Hamid's feet. His tears glistened on Hamid's black shoes. He mumbled gibberish. He stank like he had not showered in a long time. He ran his grimy hands across his overgrown, dandruff-rich hair. We could smell a strong whiff of alcohol and glue in his breath.

When Ismael held his shoulders and gave him a tight jerk and asked him what the matter was, he finally revealed the truth, which made us forget about the heat breathing down on us.

The night before Bilal's death, Saif and his friends had locked him up in the derelict hut behind the house where they often smoked beedis and drank alcohol. As usual, Sohail joined the group, getting drunk with them, mocking Bilal, calling him things like 'Pakistani pig' and 'half-witted traitor'. They asked Sohail to force Bilal into smoking a beedi. As he got up from his stool and shoved the beedi into his mouth, Bilal spat it out, his saliva coating Sohail's finger. Rubbing it against Bilal's hair, he planted a tight slap on his cheek. He fell to the ground while the rest laughed. 'Beat the dog!' they cheered him on, throatily laughing like gibbons. Sohail unleashed a spree of kicks until his toes hurt. Then Saif got up from the cot, dropping the alcohol bottle on the ground, 'Look at what I do, friends. Carefully look.'

He produced a small blade from his breast pocket, unwrapped it and headed towards Bilal, the dim, flickering light from the lantern dancing on the wall behind. Sohail froze as Bilal moaned in pain while Saif shaved off his eyebrows with the blade. The others shouted 'Woaaah!' and clapped. Some thumped the ground with their bottles in excitement. Bilal grabbed Saif's collar once the shaving was complete. He roared and punched him in the belly. Then he pulled his hair and scratched his face. Saif's friends, initially shocked, ran towards the scene and pummelled Bilal. Sohail ran out the door and threw up on the adjacent jackfruit tree's bark, his ribs hurting, before fainting.

The next morning, he woke up in the empty shack. His arms, face, and ears, swollen with red dots, itched and pained. One black ant dangled from his right earlobe. When he walked out of the shack, noises from inside the house floated up to him. He ran inside to find Bilal getting slaps and kicks from Zainab and Musa in the living room. With his eyebrows gone and black wounds all over his face and hands, Bilal looked like a creature lost on a different planet.

'How dare you hit my son?'

'Know your place, you lowlife!'

At the entrance, Saif smoked and watched the scene with a calm gaze.

'Let's teach this Pakistani a lesson for hitting our son.'

We stared at Sohail, speechless. It felt as if the ground beneath our feet would crack from the chill that sprinted across our bodies. A cool breeze crept past us, making the beads of sweat on our skin crash down. The sky grumbled.

The Maid in Dhanmondi

When the Foundation was recruiting Bangladeshi-origin photographers, writers and translators from the UK for their Women's Centre in Bangladesh for a contract of six months, Farah realized that Allah was giving her a chance to honour the legacy of Zafar, her husband slain in the Liberation War two years ago. She promptly compiled her reported pieces of three years for *The Guardian*, *TIME* and *The Times* into a thick bundle alongside her journalism school grades and dropped it on the reception desk at their office on Oxford Street. After they selected her in the six-member batch, Baba summoned their local imam in the house and invited all the Muslim neighbours for a prayer session so her daughter's undertaking would be a success. If that wasn't enough, Farah's embarrassment was compounded by the long spread of Afghan and Bangladeshi cuisines in the backyard. Their aroma swirled in the air and gripped the neighbourhood in its claws of spices and smoke. She felt like she was getting married for the second time. She saw some aunties and cousins roll their eyes and shrink their noses when Baba ended the program, his eyes full of tears and with a speech, saying how proud he was of his little daughter whose devotion to her country made him respect her more than his late mother. She knew after which words his tears would come down, after which words he would pause a little. The speech, the intention, the emotions, all of these were genuine, no doubt. She ought to love him for his fatherly affection. But because he repeated his actions every time she did something big, like when her articles on the Bangali people's self-determination pre-war and during the war were published by the 'hi-fi' magazines as Baba liked to call them, she was repulsed by the idea of being the subject of public display. To her, standing on a public podium meant exposure to jealousy-riddled evil eyes. Growing up, her Islam teacher warned her to be careful about flaunting one's blessings in public. 'The evil eye... it's such a dangerous thing. Many people don't believe in its existence but it's their loss!' the sombre looking teacher had said after she saw Farah parade around the neighbourhood with the new bicycle she had received as a birthday gift.

From the aeroplane window, the capital seemed like a flooded plain. The expansive lakes merging with rivers and roads and paddy fields confused her. Her spirit wafted out of her body and inspected the water and the fields: Were Zafar's remains anywhere in those places? Goosebumps electrified her. She was in a place where she was born but had no memory of, because Baba and Ammu moved with her to England when she was five. She was in a place where her husband was martyred after leaving his medical practice in London to devote himself to the cause of liberation.

At the Tejgaon Airport, she got inside an Ambassador that the Foundation had arranged with two other members of the cohort, Claire and Andrea, who happened to be her juniors from the journalism school. While they were busy clicking photographs of the heaps of garbage, cows, carts, vans, street children and bare-bodied men selling vegetables and toys, she looked at the smoky buildings and the bullet-holed walls and thought, with awe, the possibility of Zafar creating one of those in an attempt to kill West Pakistani soldiers.

Andrea offered if she would like to stay with them at her diplomat stepfather's bungalow inside the University of Dhaka campus. 'Claire is staying. It will be a fun all-girls "vacation" for six months!' she said as she pushed her sunglasses over her hair. 'Actually, I have other arrangements. I am sorry. But no worries! We will meet at work every day,' Farah replied. Andrea laughed. 'Right. No worries.'

She worried at first, what if the duo were thinking she was too arrogant to accept their proposal. She thought of asking them at the office if the offer was still on. But after her first night alone in the Dhanmondi bungalow, her childhood home that had been swept and dusted inch to inch by Uncle Abdullah's servants, she dismissed her feelings. She was not here to bond with the same kind of people she could easily find back home. She wanted to immerse herself in her Bangladeshi roots for these six months and feel a fraction of what Zafar must have felt after tying himself to his country of birth with utmost loyalty.

Uncle Abdullah was Baba's best friend from his Cambridge days. He was now a Member of Parliament. He loaded Farah's ears with stories of how she would expect candies from him and his wife with pleading eyes and raised palms whenever they visited the bungalow (which was quite often because Uncle Abdullah's residence was just two bungalows away), how she would mimic the roaring of tigers when they were staying at a colonial cabin deep inside a national forest in Tangail, how she would build towers with Baba's engineering books.

Given the history of familial friendship and the urge to connect with her *own* people, she didn't refuse when Aunt Shazia offered Farah a full-time maid at lunch on the second day of her arrival.

*

Naznin was five years younger than Farah. She was talkative and loud. She sang while cooking and doing the dishes and laundry when Farah wasn't home. She flew kites on the rooftop in the afternoons. She developed friendships with other maids in the neighbourhood during her daily morning excursion to the communal bins at the end of the lane. She smoked cigarettes and ganja with them under the mango trees lining the field. On the nights Farah worked late, Naznin drank the Jack Daniel's her friends had stolen from their employers' wood-panelled study rooms.

She thought Farah's Bangla would be broken, like the foreigners' awkward massacring of the language. She was pleasantly surprised at how fluent Farah turned out to be. This inspired respect for her. It swelled when Farah told her that she must not eat on the kitchen floor but at the dining table and she must not delay her dinner time by waiting for Farah to finish first.

The first few dinner sessions were uncomfortable for Naznin. She felt self-aware. Was Farah judging the way she picked the bones from her trout? The way she made and raised a ball of rice mixed with bits of fish into her mouth? Was her mouth making too much noise from chewing?

The discomfort dissipated when Farah asked her to sit beside her on the couch and chatted with her late into the night.

'Where does your family live?' Farah started with the most basic question.

'Narayanganj,' she replied, her eyes on her clasped fingers.

'Have you worked in Dhaka before?'

'No, ma'am.'

Farah threw her head back and laughed.

'You don't have to call me that. And you are so stiff! Loosen up a little. I am not a monster.'

'Um – and where are you from, ma'am? Sorry, not ma'am...'

'Call me Farah. And I was born here, but I have lived in England with my Baba and Ammu my entire life.'

'That means you move around with the *bideshis*?'

'Hahaha. Yes, I do.'

'Do you eat *bideshi* food always? Do you get Bangali food there? How does it taste?'

'*Bideshi* food, sometimes, especially when I am outside. But Ammu and my neighbours cook Bangali dishes really well, so I often eat those.'

Naznin stared at the TV's blank screen as if anticipating someone's arrival out of it. Farah moved her tongue over her upper teeth.

'You tell me. Any brothers? Sisters?' Farah began again.

'I have two sisters. Farzin and Shaznin. They're younger than me. Twins, too!'

'That's amazing! I knew a pair of twins back in high school.'

Naznin shook her head, smiling. Then she threw her gaze back at the TV.

Farah wanted to ask more about her family members in Narayanganj to shatter the awkward silence punctuated by the croaking of frogs outside but decided against it, thinking that might be too inquisitive. If Naznin wanted to share, she would do so in due time, Farah thought.

'Anyway,' Farah said. 'I think we should be friends.' She extended her hand. It was a calculated decision. Yet, she felt an unexpected jerk beneath the legs. In Bangladesh, Farah did not want to move around in the circle of people she knew through work or family. She wanted to be near people who were different from the ones she often socialized with. She intended her action to be an echo of Zafar's. She imagined how he must have laughed, hugged and joked with the fishermen, farmers, blacksmiths and rickshaw pullers in the countryside after blowing up a camp or two as their guns lay scattered around a bonfire.

Naznin, taken aback by the abruptness of it, stared at her eyes for a while and extended hers as well.

By the next night, Naznin was emboldened by hours of practice. She had imagined the empty aquarium beside the stairs to be Farah and made informal conversations with it:

'Hi, Farah. Did you get your periods this month?'

'Hi, Farah. What do your parents do?'

'Hi, Farah. Do you think this dress is too tight for me?'

'Hi, Farah. Currently, I am craving love. I want a man. Can you look for a *bideshi* man for me so I can get out of this country?'

'Hi, Farah. Can you take me to England? I really want to experience how one must feel up in the air!'

Farah was just rolling up her prayer mat in her pink billowy *khimar* she had reserved for the purpose. Naznin saw her through the slight opening of the door. She used to think people forgot god once they left their homeland. When Farah went to office in a burkha, Naznin's eyes shot up. The fact that a woman who had lived in England all her life could wear a burkha every time she went out poked her chest. She counted to three and entered the room without knocking, anticipating the execution of her practice.

'Farah. Can I ask you something?'

She felt her mouth loosen and fall off her face because she was so accustomed to addressing city women as ma'am.

'Yes, sure. You don't have to ask when you want to speak.'

'Is your husband a *bideshi* too?'

Farah paused for a while. She fingered the furry fringes of her prayer mat.

'No. He was a Bangladeshi.'

'Was?'

'Yes. He died in the war.'

Naznin could not register.

'So, he... he lived here?'

'No, no. He came from England to fight.'

It sounded surreal to Naznin's senses that a man living in such a big country would sacrifice everything and come so far to fight for a small country that had been plundered of its resources by West Pakistan.

'*Ach*. I'm sorry. I didn't...'

'No, don't worry. It's okay.' Farah dabbed the corners of her eyes with the loose end of her sleeve.

'Whenever you are sad, you can speak to me, okay?'

'Okay, I will.' Farah snorted and laughed, the bedroom's yellow light reflecting off her tears.

In the morning, Farah followed Naznin down the driveway. It was a Sunday. Naznin was just opening the gate to look for a rickshaw when Farah said, 'Wait for me!'

Naznin's neck slid back. 'But ma'am – sorry, Farah – I am going to the meat market.'

'Doesn't matter. I am going with you.'

'It's very... how do I say? It's very smelly. Can you handle it?'

'C'mon, Naznin. Don't worry about me. Let's go.'

The market was different from London's meat markets. Here, the ground was wet with puddles of rainwater and blood. Flies were a constant companion. The smell of entrails colonized Farah's nose. She threw up into a bin filled with hoofs and eyes while Naznin eyed a goat's leg to ascertain whether it was meaty enough.

'See? I told you!' She stroked Farah's back as she heaved into the bin still.

Once out, Farah held Naznin's hand and led her towards the man selling *jhaalmuri* beneath the utility pole.

'I don't think you should—'

'Relax, Naznin! I will be fine. There's no smell here.'

The man slid chopped onions, chillies and coriander into a red mug. Then he scattered four handfuls of puffed rice before mixing everything up with a final touch of mashed chickpeas. The *jhaalmuri* here tasted much better than the ones Ammu and other Bangladeshi aunties back in London made. Was Zafar able to taste this orchestra of spices? Maybe one of the fighters made one quickly before their next operation?

'Do you enjoy it?' Naznin was finishing the last clumps.

'Yes, yes. Definitely.' Farah stuck her tongue out. Her cheeks were red.

A few days later, on a Saturday, as Farah flipped through the local Bangla newspaper in the front yard in a white lounger under the coconut tree, Naznin rushed out of the house and sat beside her.

'Please don't mind, but...'

'You are being stiff again.'

'Okay, I'm telling you. Just don't judge me, okay?'

'I won't.'

'Your Uncle Abdullah. I think I am in love with his driver.' Naznin pushed strands of hair behind her ears. Farah grabbed a handful of salted peanuts from the plastic bowl on her lap.

'Do you think I should confess? Sorry I am telling you all this. It's just that I cannot keep my feelings to myself for too long. It's like I must talk to others about them. You know, back home, Ma used to pinch me sometimes for this.'

'Naznin. You don't have to explain yourself. You are my friend.'

'Correct.'

'I think you should confess first. But be careful. Don't go ahead with the romance if he doesn't propose a marriage, religiously speaking. A lot of times, guys tend to take advantage of innocent girls and spit them out after they have had their fill, you know.'

Naznin lowered her head, unsure whether she would take Farah's advice. She wasn't feeling the idea of a marriage in her bones yet. She decided to not let Farah know that she would ultimately be pursuing a non-serious relationship.

'With my husband, it was me who had proposed first. He lived in our neighbourhood. I first saw him when he came to help Ammu with the tap in her garden! I wish I could show you a photograph. He was so damn handsome!'

'I'm sure he is in a better place now,' Naznin replied with a wide smile, placing her hands on Farah's. She couldn't figure what else to say.

'We can only pray and hope,' Farah replied. 'Anyway. So, I couldn't take my eyes off him. I think it was because of the way his beard sort of brightened up his face. How do I even explain? I don't know about you, but I prefer men with thick beards.'

'Aye. Me too!' Naznin raised her hand for a high-five. Farah responded.

'Then I asked my Baba to find his information through the neighbourhood uncles. And it turned out he was not only a medical school graduate but also one of our oldest imams' only son! So, imagine our happiness, considering we are from a religious household.'

'And then?'

'Then Baba sent him a proposal, and we got married.'

'Wow. I wish Allah made it this smooth for everyone.'

'I wish.'

*

In the morning, Naznin dragged a chair beside Farah at the dining table and wept.

'What's wrong?' Farah placed her hands on Naznin's shoulders.

'I saw a nightmare. I feel scared. What if it turns out to be true?'

'It won't, Insha'Allah. Just say *Audhu Billahi Minashaitanir Rajeem* (I seek refuge in Allah from the Shaytan), and you will be fine.'

'I don't think I'll be fine.'

'Why not?'

'I have been seeing the same thing once every while ever since the war.'

'Well, what is it?'

'My mother lost her legs when the army bombed our homes. I see it happening to me. It just feels so real!'

'Ahh. I'm so sorry.' Farah patted her back and stroked her hair.

After breakfast, Farah decided Naznin should come with her to Ramna Park to clear her head. They would bring a picnic basket and have lunch there. Naznin beamed at the idea. Until then, she had only seen rich people – foreigners, especially – do that with their families at the neighbourhood field.

As they got inside the maroon Peugeot Farah had rented for six months from an automobile shop in Siddheshwari, Naznin bounced in her seat. This was the first time she was inside a car. That too, a car driven by a woman.

At the park, Farah unrolled the pink-striped mat on a somewhat even patch of grass under a wood-apple tree. *Mynahs* and *shaliks* descended around them, picked at the earth, took flight and continued the cycle. Cats and dogs stretched themselves on the warm and golden grass. Men selling nuts, betel leaves, balloons and flutes roamed the area and attracted customers in singsong voices. Naznin brought the picnic basket from the trunk. In a bid to embolden herself in the friendship a step further, she brought out a bottle of Jack Daniel's and offered it to Farah.

'Let's try it! It's just one day.'

Farah's mouth was a circle.

'No. I don't drink. You know it very well.'

A coldness emerged in her voice.

'I know, but it's just one day! Cheers!'

'No... and Naznin. I didn't know you drank. You never told me.'

'Well. I was scared to be honest. I thought you would not be friends with me if you found out.'

'I thought we were being honest with each other.'

'Okay, I'm sorry.' Naznin held her ears and crinkled her lips downwards in an attempt to melt Farah with a childlike stunt.

'It's okay. Just don't hide such things from me, okay?'

'Right. In that case, you should know that sometimes I smoke as well. With the other maids in the neighbourhood. I think you and I should do it sometime on the rooftop under a full moon. It would be so much fun!'

'No. And please don't offer me things you know I don't engage in.'

The outing was brief and awkward owing to the coldness that crept up in Farah's disposition involuntarily. She felt betrayed by Naznin's withholding. She felt as though Naznin were a completely different person than the one she had befriended. Most of the sandwiches, *shingaras*, and *samochas* remained untouched. Naznin tried to converse by floating topics such as England, money, kids, men, marriage, periods, mothers-in-law and so on. But Farah's curt replies sapped her energy. The ride home was boiling with silence.

'Hi, Naznin.' Farah knocked on Naznin's bedroom door downstairs.

'Hi, Farah. Do you need anything?'

'No. Look. I just want to say sorry for whatever happened today.'

Naznin shook her head lightly and wrapped the end of her *orna* around her index finger.

'I just... I just felt slightly betrayed, you know. I felt like you were this completely different person.'

'Oh. Okay. I don't know what to say.'

'You don't have to say anything. Just forgive me. It was my fault. I shouldn't have reacted that way. But from now on, I'll be mindful.'

'No worries! You are forgiven, my child.'

They laughed and clasped their hands together as though they had just thrown a water balloon at an unsuspecting passer-by.

Farah returned early from work. It was 8 p.m. Naznin wasn't home. She didn't let negative thoughts about Naznin perforate her mind. She was famished, so she busied herself at the kitchen in making sandwiches. When she opened the dustbin to dump the onion and vegetable skins, she found a cluster of used joints. She scoffed. Why didn't Naznin tell her at the park that she didn't just smoke cigarettes but joints too? She ate the sandwiches and unlocked the door for Naznin to enter whenever she came. She didn't care should a robber steal every valuable from the house or do unthinkable things like assault and murder. Her mind was occupied with fury. As she bounded upstairs, she caught a glance of Naznin through the big square window at the first landing. She was talking with a man in a full-sleeved white shirt. It was Uncle Abdullah's driver. Now she was holding his hands. He stroked her neck. They hugged. Farah discontinued watching and locked her bedroom door.

'Farah. Why did you not lock the door? I am sorry, I was outside. I had gone to meet my friends. I thought you would be home at 9 like always.'

'I didn't? Ohh. I need to be more careful from now. You don't have to apologize. You are not my slave!'

Naznin squinted while sipping her morning tea at the table. Beside her, Farah lowered her neck to highlight some tough Bangla words on the newspaper with her pen. It was out of Farah's character to be that careless, Naznin thought. She wished human beings were simpler animals.

Farah returned early again. Not because she had an agenda to uncover more of Naznin's secrets but because she wanted to pop some sleeping pills and forget about the world briefly. Today she had interviewed a woman at the Women's Centre who was abducted by the Pakistani military during the war.

When she returned to her husband, he beat her with a cane 'for enjoying the devils' and locked her up for a few days before selling her to a brothel in Daulatdia. She escaped the narrow alleys of that maze-like place and hopped on a bus en route to the capital. The Centre was always bloated with similar stories. Biological parents, parents-in-law, spouses, cousins, uncles, aunts, friends, everyone turned out to be betrayers in those stories because they felt they had lost their honour due to the abductions and rapes. In one case, a woman's ex-husband had chopped off her nose because she went to his house late at night, demanding he return her three-year-old boy. In another case, a woman's mother-in-law had burnt her cheeks and hands with a hot cooking spud. This woman's story shook open Farah's bottled-up grief that she had been holding inside her so she could do her work properly instead of getting carried away by emotions.

She was passing by the dining room when she heard a soft flow of laughter wafting from Naznin's room. She peeked through the slight opening and saw Uncle Abdullah's driver's white shirt and Naznin's green salwar on the floor. She quietly retired to her room.

Farah writhed in her bed, unable to sleep. Should she tell Naznin off because she felt uncomfortable that Naznin had secretly brought her lover inside the house? She felt selfish for thinking about her personal relationship instead of praying for the women back at the Centre. She raised her hands to supplicate to Allah. She requested Him to make their lives easy and bring them peace and grant them the highest level of Paradise. In the corners of her mind, the issue of Naznin bounced up and down. She barely felt the prayers inside her heart.

'I thought you were not keeping more secrets from me, Naznin.' Farah slammed her English translation of Kazi

Nazrul's poetry collection on the table when Naznin emerged from the kitchen with a tray.

'What's wrong, Farah?'

'I saw him. You brought your lover inside the house without my permission. I also found your used joints in the dustbin the other day. Aren't you crossing your limits? You told me you would be very transparent with me. Is this how you pay me back for trusting you?'

The steel tray with the teacups shook in Naznin's hands. She placed it on the table and rubbed her palms on the wooden back of a chair.

'I'm sorry. I won't do it again.'

'Don't make fake promises again. Don't lie to me, Naznin. I know very well you won't listen to me.'

'No. I wi—'

Farah pushed her chair hard. It fell on the mosaic and made them wince. She grabbed her book and newspaper and charged towards the backyard as though she had an enemy to kill.

*

'Sweetheart. Why wouldn't you listen to me?' Habib said to Naznin as they lay on the cot and smoked a joint in turns on the bungalow's rooftop.

'I am not a backstabber.'

'Oooh okay. So suddenly she is more important to you than me?'

'I didn't say that.'

'Then why don't you simply steal some cash out of her cupboard and meet me at the train station?'

Naznin turned her face away and exhaled a thin trail of smoke.

'You don't trust me?'

'Aye! Stop speaking nonsense.' She slapped his arm.

'What nonsense? Do you think she will snoop around the whole country to hunt you down and get her money back?'

Naznin looked at the plump clouds in the sky.

'How many times should I tell you that I have paid the smuggler from my savings for you to cross the border into India? All you need to do is bring some cash so we can use it in case of emergency. We can live happily in that country! We won't have to be poor over there, don't you understand?'

'You weren't like this before. What on earth possessed you? You are going there legally. Your boss knows you are going. How much of a coward are you to be taking me this way, huh? What's the guarantee I won't be kidnapped on my way? I'm sure you wouldn't bat an eye then because you would be busy chasing money!' Naznin sat up.

He grabbed the back of her neck. His nails grazed her skin. He pushed her off the cot. She spat on his face. He thumped her collarbone with his left leg.

She got up, gathering her *orna* and adjusting her salwar kameez.

'It's over. Rot in hell.' She ran down the stairs, pressing her palm to her mouth.

As Farah got out of her Peugeot, someone rapped the main gate thrice. She saw a woman's sandals with embossed flowers through the empty space below. 'Who is it?' she asked, making her way forward. 'Ma'am, please open the door. I am a new maid at the house to your opposite. I have something important to share.'

'Assalamualaikum,' Farah said through the flap.

'Walaikumassalam, ma'am. Naznin works here, right?'

'Yes, she does. Why?'

'Ma'am, I don't think you know it. But actually...' The woman let out a puff of air.

'What?' Farah fingered the cold edges of her car keys.

'Her brother is a war criminal. He's infamous back in our village for this. He is a traitor! He was with the Razakars. That devil betrayed his own country folks.'

'What? Why should I believe you?' Flashes lashed from the corners of Farah's vision.

'It's up to you, ma'am. I'm telling you for your own good. You can ask the delivery man at the post office. He is also from our village. Ask the butchers at the market behind the lake. They are all from our village, ma'am.'

Farah's head turned light as though her skull were holding an echoing emptiness inside. A chill zigzagged across her back. She was thinking of Zafar. Could it be that Naznin's brother was his killer? No, that would be an extraordinary level of coincidence. She was thinking of people like Zafar, like those women at the Centre. She thought how they all had to suffer because of the West Pakistani military and their collaborators.

The woman left her to process the news alone.

'Didn't you say your mother's legs were blown off?'

'Yes. Why?'

'Really? How so?'

'What do you mean?'

'Your brother is a war criminal! A traitor!'

'Wait—what are you saying?'

'Don't act so innocent, Naznin.'

Farah's face was red. She slid her dinner plate off the table.

'Answer me, Naznin!'

Naznin's first instinct was to lie. But she didn't want to withhold anymore. If this was a real friendship, Farah would forgive her for one last time and let her keep the job, she thought.

'Yes, my brother was with the Razakars,' she said in a muffled tone. 'But you know why? Because he wanted to have my mother treated at the military hospital! He also wanted to protect me and my sisters from the military monsters!'

'Oh, okay. I am sure that makes it absolutely okay for him to help terrorize other innocent people.'

'I'm sorry. I'm not speaking in favour of him. I am just hoping you will understand why I didn't tell you anything about it.'

'What's there to understand, Naznin? Do you even realize how shameless you are? You have been living under the same roof as me despite knowing that my husband died because of the military and yet you have been gutsy enough to hold on to your secret.'

Naznin shook as she wailed. She pressed her temples, as if to make everything stop existing for some time.

'My husband. He was such a generous and loving man. I miss you, Zafar. I miss you so damn much.' Farah held the edge of the table as she lowered herself on the ground. 'God, I feel like I am dishonouring his death for having you live in this house!'

'Farah. Who told you this? Please tell me.' Naznin neared her. She stopped when the idea of Farah's potential violence alarmed her.

'I don't want to talk.'

'Farah. Please. Please tell me who it was.'

Farah was walking out of the dining room towards the staircase when Naznin grabbed her wrist.

'Please tell me, Farah. I beg of you.' She fell at her feet, wrapping her arms around her legs.

'You can stay here for the night. I want you gone tomorrow morning.' Farah shook her legs free and went upstairs. All night, Farah wondered how foolish she had been to take the friendship seriously. People like Farah weren't meant to be close to people like Naznin no matter how hard they tried, she thought. Naznin could have easily stolen from Farah and executed Hamid's plan.

It was 11 a.m. Hamid must be halfway to India by now, Naznin thought. She dragged her bloated maroon bag through the driveway all alone. She gasped for breath several times on her way from the bungalow until the gate. She scanned its veranda and windows, looking for Farah, hopeful that, perhaps, Farah would be sad and secretly watching her leave. She paced around the gate for five minutes, still inspecting. Giving up, she opened the gate and groaned that there were no rickshaws around. She would have to walk to the end of the lane under the blazing sun.

A creak from the gate of the opposite compound.

Isn't that Aminah? Naznin squinted. Yes, it was Aminah from her village. The silver nose pin, the pink bangles. It couldn't be anyone else. She dropped her bag on the grass beside the gate and sprinted towards her.

'What did you say to her?'

'Wow. You weren't kicked out already? That's very generous of the ma'am.'

'What did you say to her?' Naznin grabbed her arm.

'The truth! What else?' Aminah scratched Naznin's hands.

'If you have any shame left, get lost quick instead of loitering here,' she added before rolling her eyes and heading towards the communal bin with a waist-level wheeled dustbin.

Naznin picked a hot rock lying at the base of the coconut tree on the footpath and hit Aminah's head. She fell on the ground. Now she hit her hands, her chest, her face. Aminah's screams pulled out drivers and maids from the other compounds. Aminah's employer's driver kicked Naznin off of Aminah. He grabbed her hair and rained a flood of slaps on her cheeks.

'Don't let this witch get away. Her brother is a Razakar!' Aminah shouted, getting up from the ground. Other maids helped her stand up, escorting her to the neighbourhood clinic.

The remaining maids and drivers murmured among themselves. They launched into assaulting her. With stones, sandals, dustbin leads. A constellation of chaos formed around Naznin. While on the ground, she found an opening between two men and slipped out of the mayhem. They chased her all the way to the gate. She limped. She didn't know for how long she could continue.

The sound drew Farah to her bedroom window. She looked out of her window to figure out what the group of people was focusing their energy on. To her, it seemed like they were beating someone up. A thief got caught, perhaps. Not something new. When Naznin was about to make her escape through the opening, the telephone on Farah's bedside table rang, making her limbs almost shoot out of position.

'Assalamualaikum?' she answered. 'Hi, Uncle! How are you?'

Crescent Boat

The newspaper is warm against Sarfaraz's fingers. Kites floating above the blue mountains in the distance fly in and out of the golden frames of his spectacles. Morris, his German Shepherd whom he named after his cranky math professor at Oxford because the canine's golden hair was no different from the scholar's, lounges beside his sleek brown cane. Outside the balcony, sparrows and swallows poke at the grass on the backyard as though they are inspecting the land for lethal weapons. Some of them take flight, gulp a small distance, cross the greying walls that resemble Sarfaraz's hair, and perch on the hippos' backs. Sarfaraz eyes Shamsie's bumpy head as she unloads pails full of watermelons, hay and grass on the hippos' muddy compound while Qazi, the man usually in charge, looks on. Shamsie, since the day of her arrival, has resolutely devoted herself to the task. Sarfaraz doesn't know the reason. He never asked. His eyes cannot maintain contact with Shamsie's. The air between them is treacherous and suffused with memories of Zeenat, his only child, who seems to drill into his soul through her daughter's eyes.

On the day Shamsie arrived with a silver trolley that battered his face with beams of the morning sun, Sarfaraz thought his seventy-year-old pair of eyes was playing mind games with him. He knew Zeenat had birthed a child twenty years ago. But the fact that this girl in front of him had the same shade of green eyes, the same curly hair and the same level of sharpness cutting across the jaws and chin charged him with flints of coal. The resemblance made his dry lips tremble. But they wouldn't curl and roll out the questions that climbed to his throat: Why was she suddenly here? How was his daughter doing? He looked at the flowers on her black pump shoes. Then her sweatshirt with Harvard splashed across the chest. And he remembered he didn't know where Zeenat had studied after the twelfth grade. He wouldn't even have known about Shamsie's birth had it not been for Ms Ashna, the new golf club's owner, whose son was the best friend of Zeenat's husband. Thanks to Ms Ashna, he was also aware that Zeenat now resides in a mental asylum up on one of the bordering hills of Sylhet. It took him around fifty minutes to travel from his estate. His eyes had turned warm with tears as he watched, from outside the cabin, Zeenat play with dolls, feed them porridge and occasionally scold them and twist their legs as punishment. A weight wilted his heart. He couldn't go inside and face her. After all, it was he who had cut off ties with her after she married Zafar. An ordinary bank employee, against the slew of proposals – army officers, navy officers, doctors, lawyers – he had in mind for her. He paced in the corridor for a while. An infrequent stream of relatives visited and left the other cabins. *Where was Zeenat's daughter?* he wondered. Two hours later, he asked the receptionist and learned that Shamsie was unaware of Zeenat's condition. She would be returning from the US today on account of her semester end vacation. After he left the building, he asked his driver to explain to the receptionist that he would take care of all the expenses. For how long could a man like Zafar afford to pay for this fancy facility? As per his prophecy, within a week he heard from Ms Ashna that Zafar had left his decades of bank service and started living in a cabin in the woods like a hairy hermit.

'Poor fella is stricken by remorse, bhaijaan,' she said while dipping a round biscuit into her tea. 'The day Zeenat's car hit the truck, the fella slapped her. Can you imagine? And all because of his twisted imagination!' His gaze stretched across the sloping golf course, empty except the receding afternoon sun. He wanted to drive to the forest, brave all the rocks and thickets and slopes, and beat Zafar with his cane. His knees, however, put a leash on his impulse. 'Why must he think that our lovely Zeenat was having affairs with her colleagues just because she is a gorgeous lady? I am telling you, bhaijaan, if my husband, may he rest in peace, was this insecure, he would have tasted my wooden spoon!' Ms Ashna droned on. He brushed aside the seed of an idea that he would visit the facility again and perhaps unite with his granddaughter. Shame and guilt grew tentacles around his legs. No, he couldn't face Shamsie either. Why must love bloom after all is lost?

*

The estate used to be a forest, spanning acre after acre until it reached the farthest lake. Sarfaraz's father Aamir, founder of a steel and timber industry, the sole heir of a landowning family in the good books of the British, cleaved eighty acres off the forest and turned the territory into their family residence, naming it Crescent Boat. To do justice to the name, he ensured the grillwork of main gate consisted of standard fist-sized crescent boats here and there. Even the cornices inside and outside the bungalow boasted crescent boats.

Aamir's wife was obsessed with hippos. She always complained that she had never seen one in real life and her brother's description of the animal from his frequent business trips to Ghana had charged up her desire. Upon her persistence, Aamir slapped his forehead. This woman couldn't pick any native animal, he thought. The British were kind enough to supply his estate with a consignment of thirty hippos (and six red and maroon Lincoln Continentals because he had secured six expansive patches of land for the British). A white granite wall was built behind the bungalow. The hippos were released on a decent swathe of grassy land that sloped downwards and met the lake. Fortunately, the lake was surrounded on all sides by the timber forests and tea plantations under the family's ownership, and as such, no villager could draw any of the hippos' blood.

Anticipation flitted inside Aamir's chest like a mob of bees when he was on his deathbed. Who should he bequeath this property to? Sarfaraz? Shafqat, Sarfaraz's twin brother? Both loved the hippos. He thought they loved the beasts because they reminded them how much their late mother had adored the beasts' writhing and muddy presence. They lived in the bungalow with their wives and children, even though Aamir thought they would live separately after marriage. They didn't hug and kiss their family folks upon returning from the factories. First, they dangled thin sheafs of grass over the walls and watched the hippos bare their buttery teeth and swirl their purple tongues. His dilemma turned out to be worthless because the twins were shrouded in an untainted gauze of love and loyalty. Since Sarfaraz was two minutes older than Shafqat, he placed his hands on Aamir's feverish knuckles and said, 'Papa, please give Crescent Boat to Sarfaraz bhai. I will take the tea estate.'

But now Sarfaraz is the sole surviving member. Sometimes, he scans the area where the hippos (only eleven remain now) mill about and hopes to find his parents and brother lurking among them. He curses his age as the bones around his shoulders ache and the thin bundles of grass fall on the mud before the hippos can grab them directly from his hand. He also curses Aamir's desire to build the bungalow on a mound for a pristine view of the blue mountains and treetops when he climbs the stairs leading to the main door and finds pieces of his heart wobbling with his knees.

To sustain his family of three generously for as long as they lived, he sold all the family land except Crescent Boat after Shafqat's family of five perished in a landslide and the family business empire crumbled because Sarfaraz couldn't hold on to their companies' ownership alone in the face of rising competition from other steel and timber industries.

*

Since Shamsie's arrival, he feels the sense of continuity comfortably sitting on his shoulders. The family blood won't end with him. The unspoken matters, however, tug at his supple skin. How much does she know about his relationship with Zeenat?

On the second day, Shamsie served him tea with a light touch of milk and seven toast biscuits on the balcony attached to his room. Mannan, the cook who was around fifty, had filled her in on the topic when she asked him about Sarfaraz's ideal breakfast. She sat on the bamboo sofa with her legs folded on the blue sofa seat. Morris lay beneath her armrest and twitched his ears whenever two yellow butterflies disturbed his peace. Sarfaraz slurped his tea and stole a glance at her.

She seemed to be engrossed in a different world. Rohinton Mistry's *A Fine Balance*, specifically. What did she want? He didn't know then that their days would be spent in silence. Breakfast, lunch, dinner. Together, in silence.

Shamsie didn't venture out of Crescent Boat much. He often found her walking the length of the walls. She fed the hippos. She sat on the wall with a cup of coffee and a novel, especially in the afternoons. Márquez. Joyce. Rushdie. Desai. Roy. He sucked his teeth and shuddered, imagining she might fall over to the dangerous side. He wanted to admonish her for being this daring.

In the mornings, he no longer found Morris lazily sleeping with his tongue out on the carpet. He now walked behind Shamsie as she, from time to time, lightly pulled the leash. They jogged around the circle of tulips and hedges in the front yard. Then they disappeared into the narrow path beneath the clump of bougainvillea and *krishnachuras*. It made him travel from one end of the house to the other with his cane rapidly tapping the floor as if that would make Morris and Shamsie slow down. When he reached the balcony opening towards the backyard, their walk turned into a jog. Now Shamsie's headphones were on. The chain on the leash remained tied with a pouch across her waist.

To dispel the halo of mystery oozing out of Shamsie's presence, Sarfaraz tried, several times, looking into her laptop where she regularly wrote – never in her room; always on the sofa facing the TV and the giant window in the living room – once evening rolled in. At times, he put Zeenat's birthday as the password. At times, he put unpredictable capitalizations of Zeenat, Zafar and Shamsie's names. When these didn't work, he thought perhaps it was Shamsie's birthday. Which he didn't know.

When she brought him his medicines before bed (a duty that she had politely snatched from Mannan), the silence felt more accusing than usual. He grinded his teeth and curled his toes. What does she know? What does she want to know? Questions sloshed in his head. Her fingers on his belly as she injected the insulin made him flinch. Made him want to relegate himself to the bunker eternally. As a child, Zeenat would run small cars over his protruding belly. The coldness of their wheels and the warmth of Zeenat's fingers would tickle him and wrench a soft stream of giggles.

Today, Sarfaraz wakes up before Shamsie. He has decided it is his turn to take Morris walking should Morris lose affinity for Sarfaraz under the haze of Shamsie's companionship. He leaves his cane on the grass. He winces with each step he attempts to run. Morris stares at him in a pleading manner. Shamsie emerges from behind in her red and white Harvard Debaters' Society tracksuit. He didn't know she is a debater. What did she debate about? He wanted to ask. He was pleased that she didn't derail her life with questionable turns like Zeenat. Her nose shrinks as she registers that Sarfaraz is out for a brisk morning walk. She strokes Morris' head. Sarafaraz allows Morris to be entertained for a few seconds before pulling at the leash and continuing what he undertook. Shamsie crosses them with her jog. Three rounds later, she hears Sarfaraz's cane thud against a paving slab behind her. She runs where he fell.

When she grabs his arms, he frees himself with a jolt. He stands up with the support of his cane. Whenever Shamsie tries to help, he waves his hands. 'Go away,' he says. Her eyes narrow, mouth widens. On the third day of his wife Zeba's death, Sarfaraz was about to slap Zeenat when she grabbed his imposing arm and kicked his shin before running upstairs and locking her room. She was mad at him for not taking her mother to the doctor who was well known in Sylhet for treating malaria fever. Instead, he had taken her to the British doctor who had just gotten his degree from the UK. He had thought the British doctor would have been better than a local.

Ever since her mother's death, Zeenat broke out in episodes of rage where she threw flower vases against the wall, dinner plates off the table, and in one instance, smeared with a bucket full of mud and cow dung Sarfaraz's library sagging with Urdu literature books. The extent of her rebellion allowed little space for grief to take complete hold of Sarfaraz. He had thought a father's first-ever slap would be enough to stop her outbursts so he could finally grieve in peace. It ended up festering Zeenat's wounds with a charged potency. She skipped her classes for months. He had mistaken this act for a natural coping mechanism. In a year, she quit school. Another slap. This time she couldn't defend herself.

'I'll make sure you suffer until your death, you colonial stooge!' she said while running scissors through the curtains in his room. He had to renovate sections of the house at least once every week. One day, she set Sarfaraz's bed on fire. Indoors and outdoors, servants rushed inside to douse it.

'What's the point of you sleeping in peace, tell me? Have you no shame after killing mother?' Zeenat poked his chest as remnants of black smoke bellowed out of the bedroom door. She was locked up in the bunker for a month. Her new friends – European hippies who had come to Sylhet to find the purpose of life – raided the estate once every three days and badgered him about her whereabouts the entire month until he had his guards beat them up with sticks – no mercy for even the three women in that group. During lockup, he arranged for lavish marriage proposals by virtue of which he would send her far away from here. He had understood that loving her from a distance would have been the best option. He was optimistic that she had changed once he released her. She mostly stayed in her room. She ate less. She broke out in tears, wailing for her mother to return. He comforted her. She never hugged him back.

Some days later, he insisted she go out with her old friends from school or the European hippies if they were still in Sylhet. A seemingly permanent smile beamed across her face when she returned from those regular excursions. Sarfaraz was happy that normalcy was beginning to grow back.

'Beta. Some people will come to see you tomorrow evening, okay?' he said, dragging a chair beside her as she wrote in her diary. 'Who?' Her eyes were fixed on the pages. 'This guy is a Navy officer. Very handsome. His family owns land in Bombay, Delhi—' Zeenat pushed her chair back. The sound sawed Sarfaraz's teeth. She didn't turn to see him. She fled inside the mosquito net and disappeared inside her blanket. In the afternoon, she brought home Zafar. Sarfaraz hadn't finished lunch. He was licking curry off his fingers.

'Papa, this is Zafar. We just got married.'

Sarfaraz threw a stern look her way. His face shuffled back and forth from Zeenat's to Zafar's. His heart threatened to come out of his mouth with a dense stream of vomit.

'What nonsense?' He stood up.

'Not nonsense, Papa. I love him. We are husband and wife. Your wish doesn't matter.'

He shook and moved his hands, trying to grasp some form of language. Why didn't you tell me sooner? He wanted to convey. 'You have crossed your limits, Zeenat!' he said when he grabbed the shore of the reality standing before him.

'You would have been much happier with a Navy officer, you fool! What does he do? Is he in the Army? A doctor?'

'I didn't know you were this cheap, Papa.' Zeenat shot back. 'He is none of those things. He is a banker.'

'Hold on. One second. So, you dumped the Navy officer for this duffer?'

'He is not a duffer. Mind your tongue, Papa.'

Sarfaraz slid out of his slippers and hit Zeenat's hands with one. Zafar, shaken at first, pushed him to the floor. Sarfaraz's eyes grew wide. 'Zeenat... look. How dare he! Look what he did. Look at the man you are calling your husband!' She didn't meet his gaze. She hugged Zafar while he stroked her reddened forearms. 'Let's go,' Zafar said.

'Fine! Go! Humiliate your father and reject a comfortable life for this *buddhoo*!' Sarfaraz shouted as they made their way out. 'And remember. You, witch, are no longer my daughter!'

Zeenat stopped for a moment. She turned back, as if to engrave his face on a memory-shaped wall. Then she walked out the gate with Zafar.

*

Shamsie cannot shake the last day off. Sarfaraz's rudeness that morning still claws at her flesh. At the dining table during dinner, she attempts to diminish the silence stretching like telephone wires between them.

'Nana.'

Sarfaraz looks up to gauge whether the voice matches her face. Her voice is nothing like Zeenat's.

'Could you please explain why you were mad at me yesterday? I'm sorry if I did anything, but are you still mad?'

A clatter of spoon, fork and fish knife from Sarfaraz.

'No. Why would I be mad?'

'Well, if you're not mad, how come you behaved like that yesterday? And you didn't speak a single word the entire time I was here. I am sorry. I am not trying to be disrespectful. I am just looking for an answer.'

Sarfaraz coughs. He drinks an entire glass of water and wipes his mouth.

'I thought you were going to speak first.' He found relief in dodging the question about yesterday.

Shamsie laughs.

'Right. I didn't because I know you and mother never contacted one another. I lacked the guts, I suppose. I was actually anxious when I showed up here. I thought you wouldn't recognize me and kick me out.'

'Ms Ashna showed me your photos. I couldn't not recognize.'

The urge to burp floats in Sarfaraz's throat. He withholds it for a while and releases it upon failure. Shamsie's eyes retreat from Sarfaraz's face and fall on the glazed lamb chop.

'So, why exactly are you here? After all these years?'

'I just want to know what happened between you two. That's all.'

'Don't you have better things to do? Young people are busy with so many rubbish things and too much free time these days!' He throws his hands in the air.

Shamsie scoffs. 'It's not rubbish, Nana. I deserve to know. I have no other family.'

'Really?' Sarfaraz's eyes turn into slits. 'No one from Zafar's side?'

'Baba grew up in an orphanage.'

Sarfaraz feels vindicated. His verdict was correct. His daughter indeed married a wretched, good-for-nothing man.

'And you couldn't ask this nonsense topic on the day you came?'

Shamsie scoffs, again. Then she looks at her nails. She is satisfied with the shine, having rid them of adamant colonies of mud in the evening.

'I told you. I lacked the guts. One cannot simply show up one day in front of a relative whom they have never seen and ask them such questions. It's awkward.'

'I thought you were a debater. Since when do they begin to feel awkward to ask questions?' Sarfaraz picks a strand of meat lodged between his teeth. Shamsie doesn't wish to entertain his dig at her skills.

'So, will you tell me?' She fingers the cold edge of her fork.

Her persistence grows warm over his ears, itches his back, drenches his armpits.

'You are one ill-mannered child, do you know that? Shameless girl. Disturbing an old man like this. No manners and respect for an elder!' Sarfaraz snaps because in this moment he sees less of Shamsie in this girl and more of Zeenat. He leaves the dining room with a slow pace and frequent hiccups, tapping his cane across the hall. 'Bloody old hag,' Shamsie texts her best friend from college, 'won't say a damn thing!'

In bed, Sarfaraz regrets his action. He has technically lost his daughter. All he has left of her is a granddaughter. He props up his pillows for comfort. Disillusioned, he takes the extra pillow out. He sweats and turns this way and that. After giving up the idea of sleeping, he sits on his rocking chair and listens to Urdu music on his gold-plated cassette player that has managed to survive nearly a decade.

Morris chases a yellow butterfly along the banister as it hides behind pink and white flowers. Two bulbuls, perched on the floodlight, screech in turns. Mannan puts the tray on the coffee table. Sarfaraz's eyes are red, itchy. He fears the lack of sleep last night may soon play with his digestive system. He lowers the newspaper slightly and mistakes Mannan for Shamsie. He remembers the bitterness with which he stewed his words last night. After finishing his breakfast, he calls for Morris. He is still busy chasing that butterfly. Sarfaraz gets up with a groan. He can feel his joints crack. The cracking sensation used to make him afraid initially even though the doctor told him it was quite normal for a man his age. Over the years, he has learned to enjoy it as one would a constant companion. If he moves fast enough, he thinks, his structure will crumble. Blue and white pills stare at him from the tea plate. He is bloated already, so he disregards them.

On reaching the railing, he scans the blue, ridged horizon. Groans, grunts, honks, squeals and snorts from the hippos buzz in the wind. He sucks his teeth and slaps his forehead. Stupid girl, he thinks as he watches Shamsie, equipped with her headphones, perform a set of burpees on the wall. She tilts to her right when she comes to a squatting position after a high jump and falls. The hippos, wet and slimy from their morning dip in the lake, approach the spot where she fell. Sarfaraz cannot locate her body because she is at the base of the wall. Sarfaraz's mouth widens. He wants to shout for Mannan. All that comes out is air, followed by a hacking cough.

The doctor flattens his lips and covers Sarfaraz's hands with his cold ones. A lady in a green smock sweeps the floor. The smell of antiseptic vibrates inside his nose. The day before Zeba's demise, Zeenat fell on the hospital stairs and scraped her left knee. Sarfaraz dipped a fat ball of cotton into a green bottle of antiseptic disinfectant and applied it to the wound.

Zeenat sank her fingers into his neck. 'It's okay, beta. Just a little longer,' he said.

'Things would have been worse if she was brought in late,' he says before patting Sarfaraz on the shoulder. Sarfaraz finds it condescending, the doctor's weak attempt at consolation. 'Worse?' Sarfaraz thinks. 'How could death be worse than a coma? If anything, death would be more final and clarifying.' He sits on the sofa inside Shamsie's cabin and watches her bandaged head and plastered arms. Tubes crowd her face. One of her eyes is purple.

'I'm sorry,' he says, his hands on her white plaster. Its hardness gives him the impression she is a toy, not a human. He knows she can't hear him. This inspires him to speak and be a different version of himself. Beneath this comfort, however, lies a current of desire; he wishes she could hear him. He keeps staring at her, the gurgling and beeping sounds from the tubes and monitors enveloping them. If Qazi hadn't seen her fall and shooed the hippos away with his flare gun, surely she would be in her grave by now. Goosebumps zap across his skin upon thinking of the many what ifs. 'Come home, my granddaughter. We will live happily at my place.' He touches her bandaged head, wondering whether this unrecognizable body is indeed Shamsie's.

Entering Zeenat's cabin, he finds her playing with a larger doll than the one he saw during his first visit. As a child, she was fascinated with dolls. Especially the ones Zeba fashioned for her using her Singer sewing machine with leftover fabric once she was done making quilts and bedsheets for the month. The room beside hers boasted dolls on every shelf. It had been a table tennis room until, on Zeenat's second birthday, Sarfaraz came upon the idea. The sturdy plastic dolls were outnumbered by Zeba's fabric-spun ones. So many eyes staring from all directions gave Sarfaraz and Zeba the creeps, but Zeenat swam like a fish in the sea of their gazes. After Zeba's death, Zeenat threw all the dolls out the room's only window. Under their weight, roses, tulips and marigolds slumped like reluctant brick carriers.

She has draped it in a red sari. She makes it hold hands with another doll donning a sherwani and turban. He sits on the bed as she positions them on a wooden horse with devotion. She only notices him when he strokes her hair. The curls bring back memories of happier times. When he would take Zeba and Zeenat to the hill stations at least thrice every year. The weekly hiking trips. The annual foreign trips. The father-daughter boat rides on the lake when they would compete against each other as to who could go the nearest to any of the hippos. The father-daughter tennis matches. Zeenat and Zeba's reluctant but loyal participation as audience in the golf tournaments where he bagged trophies consistently.

'Will you play with me, uncle?' Zeenat shakes his knees, pointing at the mound of pink and silver cooking toys. 'Please? I'll make *khichuri* and *kheer*! Come, come.'

Despite the pain in his waist and knees, he sits on the floor and crawls towards the mound as Zeenat claps and giggles. 'Okay, first, we must clean all these dirty dishes. We don't want our guests to have food poisoning.' She roars with laughter now. Sarfaraz touches her chin and a smile widens his face.

'I've missed you, Zeenat.'

'Really? Why, uncle?'

'I'm not your uncle. I am your father. You probably don't remember me.' Sarfaraz anticipates these words might magically pour normalcy upon their lives.

'No, uncle! You are wrong. My father died long ago. Do you know he had hippos? Lots of them. They killed him.' Zeenat's face doesn't display any distortion, any wrinkle of pain, memory. Sarfaraz wishes he were dead, as per Zeenat's imagination. Separation through death must be better than separation through memory, he thinks as his legs turn cold.

She busies herself with imaginary washing and cooking. He caresses her head, his joints still aching and urging him to sit on the bed or sofa. Zeenat stirs invisible cooking elements with a small pink spoon. Her tongue is out. Like it would often be when she solved puzzles or did math problems. If the green ribbon holding her hair in a ponytail were maroon, he would think something hurled him back into the past.

Tresses of water spill down his eyes and fall on a toy plate. 'Ahha, don't make these wet, uncle! I can't serve my guests in wet plates.' She takes the plate and wipes it with her sleeve, urgency coursing in her movements.

Indira Road

You leave for Dhaka from Kushtia because Hasib, your roommate at the madrasa whose family lives on Indira Road like yours used to, tells you that the apartment building of your childhood will be torn down soon, and a hospital will spring up in its stead. You owe the place a last visit. Not for your Baba, not for your Dadi, but for your Ammu. You don't know if any of them are alive. It's Ammu's memory that wrests your legs towards the past. It has been five years since you last saw the building. Back then, Bangladesh was still East Pakistan.

The rusty and croaking bus enters the city just before dusk. At the crowded bus stand, the Maghrib azan shrouds your body like fog. Before taking a rickshaw, you buy a roasted corn from one of the many vendors. Buses unload passengers and they lurch towards those men in waves. Roasted corn was Ammu's favourite. She bought four daily from the man who, every afternoon, rattled the neighbourhood in a singsong voice accompanied by mild drum beats. She kept three for herself and one for you because you couldn't handle that many roasted corns. As the rickshaw hurtles inside the city, you observe how so much has changed. Olive tanks don't stand guard on the roads. There are no remnants of Urdu-speaking soldiers in khaki uniforms and frequent checkpoints fortified with guns, jeeps and sandbags. No piles of corpses. No vultures hovering above them. There are buildings under construction. Your neck hurts as you count how many storeys each has. Sleepy employees ride home on tin-like buses that thrum with limbs. People dangle from the doorways. Some men are in relative comfort as they swoosh down the roads on their Vespas and Lambrettas.

The park on Khamar Bari Road has walls around the boundaries now. The darkness prohibits you from making out the trees. Their sibilant whispers in the breeze hurl you back to the night you left home. You heard the same whispers then. The rickshaw then turns left, staggers in a puddle and enters Indira Road. Your breath grows thin when the grove of coconut trees welcomes you. Your neighbourhood is the same as before. The lighting still sparse. A few dots of orange spilling from lamp posts here and there. It remains pregnant with inactivity. Some houses are unpopulated, their windows broken. Some bear bullet holes. Some have had their upper floors reconstructed for people to move back after the Indian air raids.

You pay the fare, dismount the rickshaw, and sense flints of cold in your legs. 'All residents: Evacuate by 16th June,' the poster hanging above the collapsible gate reads. It seems everyone has evacuated already because the lights are out except the landlady's on the ground floor. You press the buzzer to her apartment. Ms Nawaz looks smaller than before. Her hair has turned white. Her steps are light and slow. She adjusts her glasses and squints. 'Oh, my goodness! Is this you, Kashem? Oh, look, how old you have grown!' She covers her mouth with her hands, the keys dangling from one. 'Here, my son. Hold the torch,' she says. She fumbles with the lock for nearly two minutes. She hugs you and rubs your back. Her tears dot your white thobe. 'You are completely unrecognizable!' She touches the sharp edge of your incipient beard.

You nod and smile. You barely have the patience to entertain her at the moment. 'I will meet you very soon. But for now, I want to go check on our apartment. Could I have the keys please?' You don't ask about where Dadi and Baba went after your departure.

'Oh, sure, my son. Here. I am sorry for keeping you blocked. Do have dinner at my place, okay?'

'Sure, aunty.'

Ms Nawaz holds her torch over your bag as you struggle to find yours from the jumble of clothes inside. She wipes tears off her face and smiles. You hear her door shut when you make it to the first landing upstairs. Your house is on the left side of the third floor. Each floor has two apartments. The stillness and the emptiness don't make you think of hideous djinns. You feel that it's just another night from the past when the building would be populated, but frequent load shedding made it seem empty like a graveyard.

You open the door, and a stench suffused with the smell of urine, leaves and gas strikes your face. The house is devoid of furniture. A cat howls upon seeing you and jumps out the living room window. The creeper plant Ammu had placed around the grilles is gone. She bought it from a nursery beside your school the day before strikes raged across East Pakistan, and schools and offices had to be shut down indefinitely.

'Doesn't it look just perfect?' she said. You had no interest in plants. You smiled for courtesy while your stomach grumbled loud enough for her to hear. 'Come, come. I'll give you lunch. I've cooked mutton today.'

You didn't sleep after lunch. The Bangla ma'am had said that there would be a class test whenever school reopened.

You had a habit of being restless until finishing a syllabus once, no matter how desultorily.

'Ammu, please hurry up!' You craned your neck towards the kitchen as you panicked before the book.

'Coming, coming!'

She wiped the sweat off her forehead and pulled out a chair beside you.

'Shameless boy! You are fifteen and still you need me to teach you Bangla? Your friends will laugh when they hear this!' She softly pinched your cheek.

'Let them! I don't care. I think you should teach them also. Our teacher isn't very good.'

For as long as you could remember, it was Ammu who taught you Bangla at home. You did well in other subjects by attending the classes. But Bangla was a tough language for you. Perhaps because you read *The Jungle Book, Peter Pan, Treasure Island* and *The Wonderful Wizard of Oz* more than you brushed up your Bangla grammar. You could not remember the rules and tricks of memorizing the grammatical methods if Ammu did not devise ways for you to retain all the information. Nearly an hour went by. Dadi came into your room.

'Aye, Ridhi,' she said.

'Yes, Ma,' Ammu got up from her chair.

You fumed at Dadi's interruption.

'Did you bring the brinjals and cabbages?' Ammu stood silent. Your concentration floated out of the book and fell into the air between them.

'No, Ma. I... forgot.' Her voice was faint.

At night, after Baba returned, he locked her inside the bedroom and beat her.

Dadi, settled like a fat crow on the couch, said to you, 'Your Ammu is so foolish. Why can't she be careful? Why does she always make me mad?' It was not an isolated incident. Yet, whenever he beat her up, you trembled with fury. On those days and nights, your prayer mat turned wet with tears.

The wall boasts islands of moulds. Some patches of concrete remain exposed. Leaves and twigs crack under your shoes. You wonder where all the furniture has gone. Where Dadi and Baba are. Are they even alive? As for Ammu, you have stopped wondering whether she's alive or dead. To you, she is dead. She is in a better world, you like to think. You pray for her after every Salah so she enjoys all the happiness this world couldn't give her. You walk into your room. Crow feathers lie where your desk used to stand. The atlas on the wall beside the veranda door is obscured by fur-like dust. Baba bought it when you got promoted to the ninth grade and stood second in the class. He showered you with kisses. He brought home five boxes of *rosogollas* and *laddoos*. For a week or so, Ammu did not have to endure his violence despite her mistakes that usually triggered him and Dadi – salty dal, chewy chicken, overcooked rice, undercooked rice, oversized *rutis*, undersized *rutis*, rotten fruits and vegetables, and the list never really ended.

You enter the veranda. Shaliks chirp from the ceiling above. You can't recall a time they did not build nests up there. Every morning, especially in winter, Ammu would place a steel bowl full of wet rice and another bowl of seeds and vegetable leaves on the floor. If you were elsewhere in the house, she would drag you into the room and together, you would peep from behind your desk as they ate. You proceed towards Baba and Ammu's room. A puddle and streaks of excrement where their bed once stood. A brown-and-white cat stares at you from the open window. You believe the room must be its lavatory now. Ammu always prayed beside the bed. You never saw Baba and Dadi pray. They never mentioned even mentioned god. When Baba had to stay outside Dhaka for the field trips his bank organized, you slept with Ammu in this room. She would ask you about everything you did at school, everything that happened at the playground just outside the neighbourhood in the afternoon. You would want to ask her questions as well. Loaded ones. Why did Baba and Dadi misbehave with her? But you never built up the courage. Often, you would find her prostrated on the prayer mat as you woke up in the middle of the night to use the washroom. You saw her sob softly into her raised hands when it took you time to fall asleep following the washroom trip. How naïve of her, you thought, to think you were asleep. Now the strongest reminder of her lies in the midnight prayers. You perform them regularly. This life becomes liveable when you raise your hands and pray for her well-being. You have a special reputation for this act at the madrasa. The imam serves you as an example to other students. 'Some of you cannot even wake up for Fajr. Look at Kashem. How wonderful he is! This young man performs the Tahajjud every night. Subhanallah,' he says.

More than half of Dadi's bedroom door has been eaten by termites. They emerged in March 1971, around the same time when your school was shut down. One afternoon, you slipped home to pick up your cricket bat because Saif's had broken after flying off his hands and landing on a pile of bricks. You saw Dadi shouting at Ammu. 'I only got my son married to a dark girl like you so that your father could bring us all the nice things he promised. Look at my door! How long have I told you to ask him for a new one?' Dadi made a slapping motion. Ammu flinched. You wanted to smash Dadi's skull with your bat.

'I've told you, Ma. I've asked him. His bakery is not doing well these days,' she said.

'His bakery hasn't been doing well for the past few years, don't you think?' Dadi swirled towards her room.

That night, Baba beat Ammu with a cooking spud. As her screams climbed into your ears, you jammed your teeth together and thought how it was god's plan to reveal the truth behind Ammu's bad marriage without your having to ask anyone about it. Ever since, you began toying with the idea that you must hurt Baba first and then Dadi for ruining Ammu's life.

After Operation Searchlight swept through Dhaka and most of your friends in the neighbourhood began leaving the city for their villages, you noticed in Ammu a boldness you had never seen before.

'Let's move, please. Mehnaz Bhabi and her family have left for Jessore. We should go there as well. That place is the safest,' she said, pressing Baba's arms.

'We are not leaving this apartment. Nothing will happen. The military will raid the villages more to flush out the freedom fighters. It's common sense!' he replied.

Gunfire sounds became common, particularly at night. Ammu shook whenever they slid into the apartment. At the end of April, there was a military raid inside the building opposite yours. Around five or six Mukti Bahini soldiers and scores of their accomplices were forced into jeeps, blindfolded. The four of you watched from the veranda in the living room.

'See? This is how unsafe the city is. Please let's leave,' Ammu said once the jeeps' rear lights faded out of view.

'Hey. Stop acting foolish,' Dadi said.

You woke up in the morning to Ammu's screams. This time Baba was beating her with a rolling pin.

Dadi touched your shoulder. 'Come, have breakfast. It will turn cold,' she said, moving towards the dining table. Your gaze was plastered to the closed bedroom door.

'Come quick, child. Don't bother about her. Your mother was saying she would leave the city with you. What else could my son do? Hasn't she turned too daring to even think of going against his decision?'

You don't enter Dadi's room. You peer into the kitchen on the right. The cabinets are half-open, empty. You proceed down the corridor towards the living room and slip. You don't know what it is. Cat urine or another type of puddle. You grab leaves from the floor and wipe your back. You rub your wet, sticky hands against the walls. Your eyes grow hot because another memory engulfs you. Memory of the day when everything changed.

You poured a healthy amount of coconut oil on the floor upon noticing that Baba was taking a shower, and he would soon come out of his room. Ammu was in the living room, massaging Dadi's feet with warm oil. You didn't have to worry about her safety. As Baba came out and fell on his buttocks, shattering the apartment with his wolf-like howling, you felt the universe align to the perfect order. Just a little more perfection was needed, you believed. And that would be achieved after Dadi was hurt. She rushed towards Baba. She held his back. 'Oh, no, my son! Nothing will happen, my son! Don't worry.'

Her face was red. She blinked her crystal-like tears away. When Ammu tried lifting him up by placing his arms around her neck, Dadi swatted her hands. 'Moron! Go to the pharmacy right now and bring an ointment!'

Ammu took her purse, slipped inside her burkha and ran. You did not offer to go because you did not want to play any role towards his healing.

Dadi sat on the floor with a wincing and moaning Baba. You were in the living room, your head buried in the newspaper. 'Hey. Come. Help me get him to the room,' Dadi said.

'I can't. Sorry, Baba. My arms have been sore since last night,' you replied.

'What an excuse!' Dadi fumed.

Gunfire rang out. Screams floated from the street below. A weight formed around your waist. You sprinted towards the veranda. A West Pakistani soldier was pulling a young girl by her hair. He kicked her midriff. Then he lifted her and threw her inside the truck. Another group of soldiers tied a few men to the poles and bayoneted their faces. Another group brought out a woman from the pharmacy. She was wearing a burkha. She was struck on the back with a bayonet. She was thrown inside the truck. She was Ammu.

In three days, you left home unannounced by joining some of your remaining neighbourhood friends who had decided to join the Mukti Bahini. You did not sign up for the fighting. Because you had friendly ties with the elders who were in their late teens on account of regularly playing cricket and football with them, they allowed to accommodate you as a non-combatant. Your goal was to search for Ammu even though you knew well that would be impossible. Even if she were alive, there were too many concentration camps bloated with captive women throughout the country to search.

You looked forward to the probable chances of getting killed in the days ahead. Many times, you fingered the cold barrel of a machine gun as the others snored into the night and thought of meeting a swift end. When they hid behind bushes as the military showered bullets from their camps, you imagined leaping out. If it weren't for Amir, you would surrender before the army and let yourself be flayed to death for what you had done to Ammu.

'Look. I can't stop you from killing yourself no matter how hard I try. If you do it, it's their win. Always remember that,' he had said when he spotted you standing by the river with a pistol on your temple. His words replayed in your head whenever you wanted to end things. A few days earlier, he had seen you scream and run north towards the army camp and nabbed you. He slapped you thrice to make you stop screaming. A confused deer chewed neem leaves behind the tussock of long grass. On the way to the Mukti Bahini camp, your chest lightened as you told him about the thoughts that stalked you.

After the war ended, you returned to Dhaka from Mymensingh with two other lucky fellows from the group who survived and inquired about Ammu at every police station and hospital. You visited the apartment in your neighbourhood several times. You always found the building empty. The other buildings around were starting to see their previous owners return, armed with sacks, trunks and beaming faces.

Foreigners took your photos as you cried while describing to police officers and relief workers how your Ammu looked. They also wrote whatever you said on their pads as they asked you about what you saw of the abduction and your following experiences in the war. You spent nearly two weeks inquiring. Then you walked towards the lake outside Farmgate flanked by paddy and corn fields. Asr azan had just finished. Its echoes bobbed in the wind. You jumped into the water.

You woke up at a makeshift hospital on a playground. You were wearing a white smock that ran up to the knees. It was made using sand-coloured tents. The smell of disinfectant and alcohol paddings pinched your nose. Stand fans whirred and stirred mosquitoes and flies away from the patients. Some of the staff members looked European. Or American.

'Do you speak English?' a woman, her hair pulled up in a loose bun, asked after a while.

'Yes.'

'Name, please?' Her face displayed concern. It made you feel as though she were Ammu.

'Kashem.'

'Please fill this out. I will see you soon. Press this buzzer if you need anything.' She crinkled her lips, lightly rapped on your shin, and moved to the patient beside you who was covered in bandages with red and brown splotches, head to toe, except the face.

Within a month, you were placed at a madrasa in Kushtia for orphans. You no longer wanted to kill yourself. You accepted the fact that your heart was now a throbbing lump of regret. It was your destiny, a lifetime of punishment, for harming Ammu.

In the afternoons, you played football with the other kids. Upon hearing their stories, you realized they had suffered much worse. Some had seen their parents and siblings burn in front of them. Some had lived in the concentration camps, forced to clean the captured women's chambers every once in a while. But you still found your suffering to be the heaviest in human history. You were able to ease into the spiritual setting because of an imam named Latif. A sturdy, long-haired man, he taught maths and led the Maghrib and Isha prayers. You rapped on his door when you wanted to talk about Ammu. He hugged you. At times, his eyes spilled as you spoke at length about the scene of her abduction. He recited verses about God testing those He loves the most with the hardest trials, verses about endless happiness in paradise. You sat on the bank behind the green dormitory building and threw your eyes on the pink and white water lilies. Butterflies and dragonflies with translucent wings settled on them, took flight. Small leaves waltzed towards the lake from the drooping tree above. A batch of three white swans swam farther from the bank, leaving a trail of ripples in which the sun wobbled. Egrets dipped their beaks into the lake and thronged the mahogany trees. These offered you a small glimpse of what Paradise might look like. Soon, you decided that Ammu was dead. And happy.

You stumble out of the apartment. You fiddle with the torch switch. Your vision is a blur as though you are under water. You press the buzzer on Ms Nawaz's door.

'Oh, my son!' she says and pulls you into a hug. 'Everything will be all right, my son. Everything will be all right.' She strokes your hair.

You break into gasps. You hold on to her like something would tear you out of this world if you let her go. Outside, the wind breathes in cool waves. The trees' whispers swallow you into the nights when you hid with the group in the forests. When they would attack one Pakistani camp after another. When they would unlock the school doors, the bunker doors. When all the women would come out and not a single one of them would turn out to be Ammu.

Unpleasant Conditions

When you wake up for Fajr every day, yawning and rubbing your eyes, the sky is dark and the first batches of crows, yellowthroats and starlings are stirring the cool air. And Ma is asleep in her room. Snoring. And by virtue of her incontinence, leaking urine.

The right side of your bed is empty. Your husband's passing will complete four years in two months. You long for him as though he has promised you that he will return and so you should keep waiting for him. After praying Fajr, reciting at least four pages of the Qur'an, and finishing your daily *adhkars* and *duas*, you sniff his clothes, which you have kept neatly arranged in his section of the closet. The only belongings of him you discarded were the sky blue shirt and the navy blue suit he was wearing that day as he drove to the hospital, excited at the prospect of not having to perform any surgeries and only attending three consecutive meetings with fellow senior doctors. The prospect remained just that – a prospect – because his car slid off the road and down it went, splitting the surface of a glistening lake, disturbing schools of fish, and *oops!* the front bumper hit a turtle's head, blinding it permanently.

Enough about your husband. That chapter of your life is a sob session. Although, to be fair, a sob session is far better in your opinion than intense rage sessions, which define your current life regarding the issue of Ma.

A month after your husband's death, she arrived at your door unannounced. At first, you did not recognize this woman with grey hair, dark skin and a garish pink cardigan over a yellow kameez.

'You don't even remember your own mother?' she said as she lugged her giant silver suitcase into your house. She seemed plumper than the last time you had seen her, which was twenty years ago. All these years, she did not receive your call once although you rang her every month. You had been wanting to cut ties with her permanently on account of her complete disregard for your existence. But the imam at your local masjid suggested you persevere, since severing ties of kinship is a major sin.

You were shocked at how this woman had managed to come all the way from Dhanmondi to your home in Southwestern Ontario. She did not clarify why she suddenly popped up in your life. You did not ask either. You were too cautious to not ruin the possibility of building a new relationship from scratch. At dinner time, you introduced her to your children, who gave each other wide-eyed looks. She hugged them, burying their faces in her powdery chest. They forced smiles throughout dinner as she enquired about their school, friends, hobbies and plans for the future. After dinner, you told your kids to never ask her about her dementia. You told them it could complicate her mental health further.

She did not have dementia. It was a lie you had made up and fed them forever because you were too ashamed to disclose the truth of your relationship with Ma. You learned the next morning that she had diabetes and arthritis as she handed you an orange file and asked you to bring the tablets listed on the paper. And it all made sense now. She wanted to spend her remaining days with her only child.

Despite the fact that her condition has existed for four years now, anxiety washes over you whenever you go into her room. Did drops of urine touch your feet? Is the tiled floor actually clean or is it hidden beneath a dry layer of urine? Oh my god. Is your Salah valid? Didn't your toe touch the floor a teeny bit that one day as you tried to rummage through her cupboard for her digital blood pressure machine? How could you be this stupid?

You have three pairs of slippers neatly arranged under the sun-like mirror outside her room. The pink one for you, and the yellow and lavender ones for your kids when the need arises to visit Ma's room. You are always cautious, so the slippers' undersides do not touch your skin or clothes. You tell your children repeatedly – at least thrice, everyday – to be armed with the same level of alertness. They wonder if you pestered them like that with regard to their grades, would they be at the top ten per cent of their class?

You head to the kitchen downstairs and defrost a batch of ten *porotas* under the running tap before frying them and storing them in a hotpot for Ma and the kids for breakfast. Sometimes you also defrost sausages, but when you are late you only make five omelettes (that too, without your usual addition of sliced tomatoes, coriander and capsicums). By this time, Ma is usually up and groggily awaiting your arrival in her bed, in a puddle of her urine more often than not. You wish Nancy, Ma's part-time Filipino caregiver who is the same age as you, could come this early because that would save you the trouble of braving the Urine Universe. You crave a full-time caregiver for Ma. Household expenses restrict you. Nancy comes for seven hours only, her shift concluding by the time you arrive.

You sprint upstairs after taking your breakfast alone at the counter, sleep tugging at your eyelids, dreading having to clean Ma up, which takes approximately an hour including cleaning the floor and changing the bedding. Besides the aching limbs and joints resulting from the activity, what angers you the most are her seemingly permanent frown and the questions upon seeing you come through the door: 'Why so late? Couldn't you hurry?' The same questions issue out of her lips every day, without the slightest change in words or tone, as though she rehearses them before sleeping.

You grit your teeth as you sponge her legs. Why are you having to take care of this ungrateful woman? You love her, no doubt, owing to the fact that she was courageous enough to show up in your life after the long absence (although without apologizing once) and the fact that she raised you all alone on a primary school teacher's income in Dhaka while your father – a Marxist, an animal rights activist, an environmentalist, a raging LSD lover and Viagra consumer – sauntered about the world and maintained zero contact (did not even care to file for divorce). But her petulant and childlike mannerisms (and needless to say, incontinence) play havoc with your sanity. You are well aware these are things that are part of the heavy package that is old age. But frustration doesn't sympathetically take matters into consideration. It simply bursts forth.

You take a bath, ridding yourself of god-knows-how-many droplets of urine that are adamantly stuck to your skin and clothes. You get ready for university, where you, as a professor, teach master's students history. You have recently started wearing long instant hijabs instead of the ones that require you to painstakingly form loops around your head and use safety pins and magnets to hold them in place.

The kids must be up by now. All the clinking and clanking of utensils floating up from downstairs. *Have they prayed Fajr?* you ask your son, Yusuf (eighteen), who is stationed on the black sofa, *Brooklyn Nine-Nine* blasting from the TV. He nods yes. You do not have to ask your eldest daughter, Fatima (twenty), who is washing her plate and coffee mug, if she performs her five daily prayers. It has been three years since she turned her life around by practising her religion with an inherent enthusiasm rather than due to your persistence. Your prayers to Allah – that may He 'please-please-pleaaase' guide your children to the straight path – were finally starting to get answered.

You kiss them both on the forehead and cheeks (a ritual you developed ever since the passing of your husband) and notice how, mashallah, Fatima's skin is always soft, but unfortunately, Yusuf's is oily.

*

You do not know what birthed Fatima's enthusiasm towards practising her faith.

The reasons are, as written in her diary, the glossy, black leather one you had gifted her when she got into Ontario Tech University:

> 28 March 2016
>
> I'm writing an entry after ages. Got an abortion two months ago, thanks to Park's mom's clinic. She was super cool about it. Although she made Park break up with me and shipped him off to Manchester to live with his father. God, I miss him. He was my only source of comfort after Baba's death. I would sneak out my window, bike to his place and

sleep with him every night. His presence made me feel... less lonely. Whenever I was with him, I felt as though grief could never hurt me. But I must stop thinking about him. I blocked him from my socials this morning. Even deleted his number. I am a true Muslim now. I don't lie to Ammu about prayers anymore. I am trying to quit drinking. In hindsight, I realise that it was Park who got me hooked to drinking. It all started with an innocent shot in his basement. Alhamdulillah, cut down drinking daily to only once every week.

Must get rid of this completely though. Otherwise... UGH. I know very well my daily prayers aren't being accepted cuz DRINKING means they won't be accepted for FORTY DAYS, OH GOD. Can't afford to die in this state and enter hellfire. No.

Besides drinking, he brainwashed me into discarding my religious identity. He brought me skinny jeans and crop tops, so I'd wear them for him under my hijab and baggy abaya despite feeling UNCOMFY AS HELL and ditch my hijab and baggy abaya in the washroom after Ammu dropped me off at school. Why do I still miss him? A guy who RUINED my life? Got to be grateful to Allah for lifting me out of the mess without letting Ammu get a whiff of things.

Only Yusuf knows Fatima's secret because she trusted him enough to tell him about the pregnancy test results on that fateful day three years ago. Well, not really. It was more like she revealed the secret in a moment of weakness, as she remained seated on the bathroom floor, the shower blasting over her at full speed, when Yusuf happened to walk in because her bedroom door was open and so was the bathroom door and he was sensible enough to moan and sigh and think of turning the shower off to prevent water wastage and there she was, a wet, hairy lump of mess.

It is not that she did not trust you enough. She just did not want to shatter your heart into a million pieces. She could not survive if the news caused you a cardiac arrest (she was sure it inevitably would) because *bam!*, then she and her brother would become orphans in a jiffy.

Aside from the gloom and doom, to look at the bright side, she has officially graduated from her drinking phase (if you got to know that any of your kids was an alcohol-fanatic, you would indeed have a cardiac arrest like Fatima assumed and depart this world and let your children rot in the bleak climate of orphanhood), approximately a year after writing that entry (April 2017, to be specific). No, not even once a week. Now, she does not have to shiver in fear when a truck carrying logs of wood passes by her car or when she is about to fall asleep or when she is about to turn the stove on (and the list goes on). A road accident? Death in sleep? An explosion in the kitchen? A myriad of other ways of death approaching and seizing her soul? No worries! Bring it on! She remains armed with *ayatul kursi* after every mandatory prayer. This means nothing can stop her from entering Paradise.

Yusuf (who, by the way, scores the highest in every class, and is planning to apply to MIT with his extraordinary debating career that has taken him across North America and Europe) has given up praying altogether. Not because of atheistic beliefs creeping up his soul but out of laziness (this non-atheism bit would give you relief if the information ever leaked itself, although the relief would be more like quenching your thirst by running into a burning house).

He finds the water too cold (despite turning the geyser on) to make proper ablution. He finds the mandatory ritual *ghusl* too burdensome. To your questions about prayers, he lies. He pretends to make ablution by cursorily splashing water over his face, hands and feet when you are folding the clean laundry in his room. He is a raging porn addict. Pen drives, memory cards and CDs full of porn. When was the last time he slept without masturbating? He is a chain-smoker. He is particularly interested in vaping. Strawberry flavour. He stole fifteen dollars from your purse to purchase a vape pen and juice. His favourite pastime includes getting high with three of his chain-smoking brothers-in-arms under the oak tree at the park while the squirrels watch (and sometimes, speak words of wisdom like 'this shan't be what thou ought to doeth with yer time, children').

He is also involved in fornication. With a white, Catholic girl. Sadie. Be happy you are as unaware as a healthy woman who doesn't know this will be her last living second. Commuting to and from work and taking care of Ma vaporizes the energy out of you. So, you really don't have much curiosity flapping in your chest whether your children have secret lives.

They obey you and that is enough, you tell yourself.

Although he doesn't pray the five mandatory Salahs, he supplicates to God to grant guidance to Sadie and convert her to Islam. He loves her. He wants to marry her. His part time job at Best Buy is enough for moving out and renting a separate flat. He would definitely marry her if she converted to Islam. But she is an unshakeable Catholic. And bringing a Catholic bride home would inevitably create rifts in the family. You, for sure, would never approve of the marriage. As for Ma, she would first disown her grandson and then telephone everyone back home in Bangladesh to convey that Yusuf has been shagging a white, *Khrishtan* girl.

At the dinner table, Ma tells you to fetch her phone from her room. 'Can I please get it after dinner, Ma?' you ask. 'Arey, how will I have my dinner without Rahim bhai's sermon on

YouTube? Now go!' she replies. You seethe, clenching and unclenching your fists.

Yusuf is not home (he is eating out with friends, or so he tells you when in fact he and Sadie are getting stoned in her bedroom). Fatima is upstairs, preparing for a mid-term exam tomorrow with her childhood best friends, Mariam and Farzin. This means you can't deploy your kids for the mission. You leave the table, the sound of the chair grating against the wooden floor sending shivers through your teeth and go upstairs. Your designated slipper for her bedroom is gone. Did Nancy leave it somewhere inside the bedroom again? You scoff, breathe heavily and bite your lips. You hesitate to take the children's designated slippers because who knows if they were as diligent as you when they went to Ma's room. You wear Fatima's, enter Ma's bathroom, and wash the slippers and your feet. Confident that the pair is now clean, you get Ma's phone and hurry downstairs.

Ma has already helped herself to a serving of dal, chicken and rice. She licks her fingers and narrows her eyes. 'The dal... tch. Why's it so salty? When did I teach you to cook such bad dal like this?' she says, a yellow smudge smeared across her chin. 'And the chicken is so stiff! Do you want to break my and the children's teeth?' she adds, her voice raised. She takes another morsel and slides her plate off the table. A ringing floats up in your ears.

You want to reply with a stream of unspoken thoughts. Thoughts only Allah knows.

Ma, the chicken and dal don't suck. They may not be perfect according to what you were used to eating back home. But don't say they suck. See these shards? I will stab you with these, you undying hag. Do you want to kill us first and then

FINALLY dig your own grave? You ungrateful pig. Ever since you descended on this house after Mahmood's death, you have been nothing but a nuisance. The only reason I am enduring your antics and not lashing out is because I fear Allah. He told us to respect our parents no matter how big of an intolerable imbecile they might be. I cannot go to hell on your own account.

You cannot touch your dinner. Your appetite is gone. You head to the kitchen, take the broom and clean the floor while Ma trudges upstairs with her bamboo stick, softly muttering words of indignation. Once she leaves, you sit on the floor and curl into a timid version of yourself, resting your back against the counter's cool marble. Tears plop on your forearms. Such incidents happen once every two or three weeks. Yet, you cannot get habituated. You long for the days when Mahmood was alive, and Ma was healthily living alone in Dhaka with no sign of diabetes and arthritis.

It is Saturday and raining outside. Fatima collects the wet clothes from the backyard. Fatima carries Yusuf's clothes on her shoulders and drops them in the laundry basket in his room. Repeated pings waft out of his phone on the desk. He is in the washroom.

The pings bother her. Fatima checks the notifications. The phone is unlocked, surprisingly. Ah, foolish brother. Text messages from Sadie Wood. A girl. Interesting. Might as well see the texts and mark as unread later. A harmless undertaking. Photos. She looks, eyebrows arched, as one after another nude keeps coming in.

The bathroom door creaks.

Fatima marks the conversation as unread, closes the app and hurriedly moves away from the desk and crouches on the floor, pretending to find a missing pen.

The door opens, and Yusuf emerges, rubbing his head with a white towel, unaware his phone was just broken into. He picks up the phone, a smile broadening across his face.

The next day, Yusuf storms into Fatima's room and smashes the flower vase (which she got as a gift from Mariam last semester) against the door. Fatima glares at a fuming Yusuf. She does not want to ask, 'What's wrong?' She sprints towards him and smacks him on the face. His nose bleeds. He kicks her on the left shin. She screams and crumbles on the floor.

'Why did you do it?' Yusuf shouts.

'What?'

'Sadie. Why did you call her and tell her to break up with me?'

Fatima stands up, adjusts her hair and stretches her shirt.

'I saw what she did,' she says. Her eyes drilling into his.

'I saw those goddamn photos, Yusuf.'

'They are none of your business.'

'They are. I can't let her lead you astray.'

'Astray, huh? Well, guess what? We haven't broken up. She was nice enough to alert me about your creepy behaviour.'

'Creepy?'

'Yes, it's nothing short of creepy to call random strangers online and lecture them about not dating your brother.'

'Wow... and practically having virtual sex is not creepy?'

'Listen, that's not the point...'

'Yusuf, just shut up, okay? I am your elder sister. You have to listen to me. She isn't going to bring you any good.'

'Don't say another word against her.'

'Why not? She's a slut, Yusuf! A slut! She has no dignity! I know such type of people. They don't want to mend their waves and they take others down with them.'

Yusuf's lips tremble. He clenches his jaws. He darts out of Fatima's room and enters your room.

'I need to tell you something, Ammu,' Yusuf says.

'What's it, honey? Oh my god, why are you crying? What happened?' You hug him. He unclutches himself from the hug.

'Your daughter. I hate her.'

'What rubbish!' you scream. 'What's wrong with you?'

'She was pregnant, Mom. And had an abortion. Back in 2016. That too, after Baba's death. While we were grieving, she was busy getting knocked up!' Yusuf says in one breath and his voice cracks. He runs to his room and slams the door shut.

Good thing Ma is asleep in her room, though. Or else, the news would make several rounds among their relatives here in Canada and back home in Bangladesh.

Your shoulders heave as you wail. You tighten your grip around the bedpost as if you are saving yourself from drowning into the floor. How is that possible? You are swimming in disbelief.

Fatima does not speak when you ask. Her gaze is fixated downwards. You jerk her shoulders as if to rattle an answer out of her.

'Why did you hide this from me? Why? Pregnant? Abortion? Who are you even?'

'Ammu... that was a long time ago,' she finally speaks, her words muffled by sobbing.

You search for something, anything on her desk. A stapler. You grab it and throw it at her. She shrieks. Drops of blood dot the tiled floor. When you look at the lacerated lips, it dawns on you that right now, you are your mother, despite the promise you had made to yourself when the children were born – that you would never become your own mother.

Memories swoop down on you like a group of vultures.

Here you are. Results day. Grade eleven. Parents' meeting. Here is Ma, slapping and pinching you in front of everyone for not scoring A+ in all subjects. Here is Ma pulling your hair and spitting on you. Ma beating you all the way home on the rickshaw with the wooden ruler while passers-by laugh and watch. Not an isolated incident. Happening since time immemorial. Here are your classmates. Throwing you chits with 'pushover' written inside.

Here you are again. You explode as she beats you with a plastic hanger for not getting into Dhaka University's D Unit. 'Why are you like this, Ma? Are you even my real mother? What under god is wrong with you?' Here is Ma again. She smacks you with the hanger on your left cheek. 'You want to know why I'm like this, you ugly slut? Because I love you! I guess it's my fault that I love you!' She pulls at your hair. The pain is non-existent on account of the other circles of ache throbbing in your hands, legs and back. 'Let me tell you this. An ugly, dark-skinned girl like you will never find a nice boy. So, you need to make a place for yourself, you idiot! For god's sake, just look at how your father left me!'

Here you are again. You get married and decide to move to Canada because your husband has a citizenship, and he wants you to have it as well. Here is Ma again. She coughs while sipping her morning tea as she hears your decision. 'You are actually going to live in that shameless country and turn into a shameless woman?' she says, wiping droplets of tea off her forearm with her *orna*. 'I knew this would happen! I knew it the moment you decided to marry that guy, paying no heed to the government service holder I brought for you!' Your gaze doesn't meet hers. Your stance remains unshakeable. Yes, you are going to fly out of your mother's shadow and build a life for yourself with your husband and make healthy babies who would receive the best parenting from you. 'Will you leave me to die alone?' she adds. You scoff and reluctantly say, 'You can come with me too, you know.' 'Why should I do that? I was born here, and I will die here. I am your mother. You are going to listen to me, not the other way round. You are already turning very bold, I see,' she says, bolting out of the room. You want to say, 'I have had enough of you, Ma. I won't let you ruin my marriage', but you don't. She refuses to return your calls from Canada. She slams the door in your face when you visit Bangladesh for the first time after moving. She repeats it for three years, and you stop visiting.

During Asr prayer, you drive to the mosque. Heavy rain hammers the roof of your car and deafens your cries. You wipe the tears from your face, but they seem endless. Your eyes sting and itch. You decide you will apologize to Fatima once you go home. But first, you need to repent to Allah for losing your temper and hitting your child for the first time in your life. If Mahmood were here, what would he think? As you drive, various stories of the Prophet Muhammad (peace be upon him) crop up in your head. Didn't he always stress the importance of controlling your rage? And being kind and generous? Didn't he say that 'A Muslim is the one who avoids harming Muslims with his tongue and hands'? Well, great. Here is more guilt. Swelling up and up. Stirring your core.

The women's section has white walls and blue carpeting. A skylight gapes on the ceiling, stationed in the centre of the room. A large rectangular TV is fitted on the eastern wall, flanked by bookshelves stretching until the end. The room is populated with eleven women excluding yourself. No familiar face here except... is that woman in the pastel burkha Sister Latifa? Forget it, you don't have the disposition to socialize.

The imam gives *iqamah*. His voice is fatherly. Comforting. Or perhaps your emotional state makes you think so. You sniff and rub your eyes with a napkin, hoping the sisters around you do not sense that you are wrecked and falling into the limitless depths of guilt.

Takbir Tahrima.

You fold your hands. You bow. Stand up. Now prostrate. Now ask for forgiveness.

A clang in the distance.

Wait. No. This can't be happening.

Gunfire sounds shroud your back. You are sooo dead today, they say. What about your kids? You want to hug them. And kiss them. And tell them you love them a lot. You want to tell Fatima that you are sorry, and you would never hit her again.

Some sisters attempt to barricade the door with the plastic, metallic and wooden chairs, but there he is. Pushing his way inside.

Bald. White. Glassy eyes. Huge mass. Straight lips. Olive jacket. Cargo pants. An AK-47 slung across his chest.

Sister one, gone. Brains wiggling on the carpet. Sister two falls on the ground. Winces, moans. And now shot in the belly. Sister three runs towards the only window in the room. Three bullets whizz through her spine before she can open it.

Your legs wobble as you bend to settle into a gap between two shelves. You fall. Blood leaks out of you and darkens the blue carpet. A stabbing pain in your abdomen. You raise your index finger and say the *Shahadah* out loud. You think of your kids. Of Ma. Of Mahmood. And your eyelids meet, wrenching you away from the world.

A Mother's Grave

Sharmin was bitten by a snake in the middle of the night. She had gotten off her cot to drink water from the earthen pitcher beside the main door. Rashid discovered her as she lay groaning and squirming on the ground. He had gone out to take a leak in the tin-walled washroom. She said, 'My son, bury me in our old neighbourhood...' before taking her *Shahadah* and closing her eyes, oblivious to the globs of snot and saliva and tears issuing out of Rashid.

Rahima, his younger sister, rushed from the town where she worked at a shoe factory the next day and saw to it that Sharmin was buried in the communal Islamic cemetery. Rashid remained unaware because he was busy lying on the patch where Sharmin took her last breath, his eyes on the thatched and cracked ceiling. Rahima dragged him and waved a plate of hot *shingaras* before his face. He wouldn't stir a limb. Her face in her hands, she cried, lamenting the death of her mother but also the fact that she would have to take care of this man whom she loved dearly but hated, too, for being the way he was.

*

Ten years ago, Rashid worked as a sweeper in Dacca, East Pakistan. Then the Liberation War rolled in, and he became a proud resident of Dhaka, Bangladesh. When his crew was assigned various roads and neighbourhood houses for clean-up operations, nothing moved him. His co-workers, on the other hand, broke down in the middle of cleaning and cursed the Pakistani military. All he wanted to do was retch because the rotten patches of blood and limbs and bones sure smelled like your entrails were dangling from your nose.

One night, he was startled awake by voices inside his head. Three of his co-workers were asleep in the small tin-roofed room they shared with one giant wooden chest but no bed. He was sweating. He pressed his palms on the sides of his head. The voices were persistent. A woman screaming. A child crying. The sound of boots and gunfire. Tanks. Bombs. He went to the veranda and lit a cigarette hoping they would fade away. They still bounced in his head as he hosed down a bloodied driveway in front of a bungalow the next morning. That evening, he resigned and received his salary from the boss. He had told him to see an exorcist. The voices, in that same pattern, continued playing in his head on the road from the capital to his village.

Upon his return, he did not see an exorcist because he did not want his mother and younger sister to think he had returned a mad man from the city. The voices stopped after a few days.

Sharmin's cow and goat were giving enough milk. For a generous stream of money, she replaced the croaking thatched roof with a new one that had tin below the thatched surface. Rahima had gotten a job as a receptionist at the shoe factory. The villagers sent *polao* and *khichuri* with roasted chicken to their house frequently. Some sent marriage proposals, which she turned down. Some girls were so jealous of her for being the first girl from the village to be this successful that they ended their friendship with her through icy silence.

He awoke one night and poked Sharmin awake.

'Tell me later. Let me sleep now, son.'

'Ma. Can you please pray for Sabrina and her son, Siam?' His face floated above her ears.

'What? Who are they?'

'They were killed in the war, Ma. Now they live inside my head. I can see them from time to time walking on the banks of Buriganga. So happy they seem! The boy holds a green kite, which, I think, is too garish but it doesn't matter. I've told Sabrina to get him a new one. They are telling me to pray for them. So, I will pray for them, and you should too.' He pulled his blanket over his head and settled into a peaceful sleep on the mattress on the ground beside a snoring Rahima. Sharmin wondered whether she was dreaming.

Sharmin woke up and realized that the encounter had indeed been a reality. She saw Rashid telling the same thing to Rahima. Rahima was feeding the chickens and twitched her lips to interrupt him, but she was unable to find the right words. She left Rashid alone with the chickens and told Sharmin that maybe her brother had lost it and maybe they should call the exorcist who lived behind the banana orchard.

The exorcist treated him for a month by forcing him to a diet of fried chillies (without rice), by subjecting him to frequent beating sessions with his dusty broom and finally gave up when Sharmin slapped the man for tearing a clump of Rashid's hair in an attempt to let the evil spirit evaporate through the bloody patch of his head.

People thronged their compound to hear Rashid speak of Sabrina and Siam like the devoted audience of a saint. Occasionally, his imagination was coloured by rosy brushstrokes.

'Sabrina is happy that the Pakistani military hasn't killed her husband! When she conveys this to Siam, he jumps and flies with the parakeets. How happy they are!'

But most of the time, it tended to be suffused with misery.

'Brothers and sisters. I feel terribly sad for them. They were so happy before the war. Living in a bungalow. Bathing with hot water during the winter. Going to the mountainside in India for vacation. Now all that is lost. I don't know how her husband is coping.'

'Sabrina told me she and her son would be very happy if I could kill at least one Pakistani soldier. But where will I find one? It will be a year soon since the war ended! Haven't all the devils left?'

'Sabrina says she needs a new *shari*. She says her white *shari* is gathering dust. But it is perfectly fine! It seems whiter than Hamid Chacha's cow! I promise! I think she is lying because she is tired of wearing the same *shari*. She is also asking me to buy ice cream cones and hair oil for Siam. That kid's hair is rough like hay, she says. I agree with her here. But the point is, when she demands these, she cries not normal tears but tears of blood! Can you imagine?'

Rahima bit the insides of her cheek whenever Rashid blurted out the contents of his head to his wide-eyed listeners who suppressed their laughter by lowering their heads and by placing their mouths into the crooks of their arms fearing Rashid might stop narrating if they made their stance obvious. Rahima wished he had died in the war instead of returning as a broken thing. Before sleeping, she calculated how Rashid's addition would strain her income from now on. She wanted to push him into the river that had swallowed their old house one stormy night before the war. She pinched herself for summoning a gruesome idea. He was her brother and she loved him except for his brokenness.

*

Rashid pushes Rahima towards the tin wall when she asks if he would like to visit Sharmin's grave at the cemetery.

'You are so stupid! Why did you do that?' Rashid prances in a circle.

'I am stupid? Brother, what are you saying? What did you expect me to do?' Rahima rubs her neck and coughs.

'Yes, you are a stupid girl. A BIG one. Mother told me she wants to be buried in our old neighbourhood!'

'Nobody lives there. It is Jubair's land. An empty land.'

'That means we can bury her there!'

'Brother, stop it for once already! She has already been buried! I will send you to the asylum if you keep behaving like this. Ever since you returned, you have robbed the joy of this household. Do you seriously not realize, or do you pretend not to?' Rahima jerks his shoulders and keeps at it.

'My dear sister. How could you say this to me? You will send your brother away?'

Rahima is silent and pushes back tears with her *orna*.

'No matter! I will go away very soon! Then I will live with Sabrina and Siam in a separate house! But if you start missing me, you can come visit us and we—'

Rahima walks out of the house, banging the door close.

'No, son. It is against the purity of the dead to do such a thing,' the imam says, his long grey beard blowing in the wind, when Rashid asks if the mosque committee can transfer Sharmin's body to their previous neighbourhood.

'But, Chacha, can you not consider my case? She tells me until I have changed her grave she cannot swim in the river when Sabrina and Siam do. She cannot eat cotton candies with them. She cannot fly like they do. She is miserable!' Rashid holds the imam's hands.

'It's all in your head, my dear. Go home and sleep. I can't guarantee you will be cured, but you ought to ignore your imaginations.'

'I can't, Chacha. You don't understand.'

At dinner, Rahima grabs his plate and throws it against the wood apple tree.

'Do you have no shame? You seriously asked the imam to dig out our mother's body? She is not even cold yet and you are thinking such things. How cruel!'

'My sister, please don't think like that. You haven't seen it, but I have. You would hate it if you could see how miserable she is. She cries while Sabrina and Siam fly on horseback. She cannot move around much! She says her hands and legs are sore.'

'I don't know what to do with you anymore.' Rahima leaves her dinner untouched and disappears into her blanket.

The next day, Rashid bikes his way to Jubair's land. The sal and mango trees scattered throughout the plot yank memories of childhood. How Rashid and Rahima would shoot at the squirrels and monkeys with their catapults and collect raw mangoes in their tin boxes after heavy rains. How Rashid used to teach Rahima the way to climb a tree. How their father died as the branch under his feet cracked while they were repairing kites on the porch.

Jubair is sitting in a plastic chair, drinking tea and speaking on the phone. 'Okay, brother, I will call you soon. Take care.' He cuts the call as soon as he sees Rashid.

'Aye, Rashid! My brother! What brings you here? How is your lovely sister? All well?'

'I need your help, Jubair. My mother. She is not happy. She is sore. She cannot walk, run, or fly. She cannot have fun with Sabrina and Siam.'

'I understand, brother.' Jubair strokes his moustache and bites his lips to not laugh out loud.

'Before she died, she told me she wants to be buried here in her old neighbourhood. She wants to be in her ancestral area.'

'Ahh. Right.'

'She tells me she will stop feeling sore if her body is placed here. So, we must hurry!'

'Of course. The thing is, I am building a paper mill here very soon. My father has put me in charge of it.' Jubair scans the river view. He throws the last sugary remains of the tea on the grass.

'I beg you, brother. You have to do something! I can't watch my mother suffer anymore!' Rashid falls on the ground and pulls at Jubair's white trousers.

'Please, please get up, brother. You don't have to beg.' Jubair brings Rashid up and hugs him. 'I will see what I can do.'

Jubair knocks on the tin door. Rahima opens it. He doesn't greet. His eyes hover across her body. 'What brings you here, brother?' she asks, stretching her green kameez as though doing so can bat his eyes away.

'Oh, I am here for your brother. May I please see him?'

'Please wait here. I will call him. He is over there near the pond.' Rahima leads him towards the cot outside. She feels his eyes pricking her back.

'No worries. I am going there then.'

'Jubair? How come you are here, my brother?' Rashid turns away from the ducks he was feeding.

'Just like that. Thought I should help out my brother.' His maroon shirt shines in the afternoon blaze like snakeskin.

'About your mother. I can certainly make an exception for you. But for that, you would need to ask Rahima to marry me. You know how I have always had my eyes on that beautiful thing, your sister! She is truly God's gift to our village, I am telling you.'

The light reflecting off Jubair's golden watch makes Rashid twitch.

'You are out of control! You should lock yourself up at an asylum. Stop messing up with my life, please!' Rahima folds her hands in front of Rashid's face like she's praying to him. Then she resumes packing her suitcase because her leave from work will be over in a day.

'But why can't you marry him? It's for mother's betterment!'

Rahima takes off her slippers and hits him as he blocks her blows with his hands. Something jolts her back. She has never hit him before.

'Why can't I marry him? Well, first of all, he is already married with two wives, and secondly, I don't want to marry him! Is that clear?'

'I am so sorry, my dear sister. Yes, it's clear. Now please forgive me.'

'Get out of my sight.'

'I won't repeat it again.'

Rashid crawls out of the house while muttering, 'Ma. Ma. Ma, I am so sorry. I am so sorry you are suffering. I am so sorry, Ma.'

Rahima zips up her bag and decides to never return.

Dogs howl and gather around Rashid as he drops his bicycle near the jackfruit tree. He walks into the maze of graves with a lantern. They follow him with pleading tongues.

By the time he finds Sharmin's grave, a faint film of dawn pushes aside the darkness. The dogs – except for one – have retired from their hope of getting treats. He hugs the grassy mound. He cries while praying for her soul. Then he swings the pickaxe into the earth. He pants. He lies down for a while. The dog licks his sweat around the uneven beard. Then he continues. He uses coppery leaves to wipe the maggots and ants off her body shrouded in a white cloth and tied at the head and feet. His face scrunches up when he lifts the body, and its putrid smell shoots up his nose. The dog howls and follows him on his way out. He sits the corpse on the back and ties it to his torso with a rope. The pickaxe and lantern swing on ropes tied around the handlebars.

He is showered with stares on the road.

'Doesn't that look like a body?'

'Could be a sack of paddy, who knows?'

'My God! I knew he was mad, but this is a new level.'

'Whose body is it?'

'O Allah! The stench is unbearable.'

'Someone knock some sense into this giant idiot.'

'Thank you so much, Allah!' he says upon discovering that Jubair (or anyone) is not here around the land. As per his plan, he will quickly finish the business, and nobody would even know. He lays the corpse carefully as though it is a cooked tilapia that would break if handled without caution. He pees a little when a hand grabs his ear from behind.

'What are you doing?' It is Jubair. He pushes Rashid to the ground. 'Were you going to secretly bury her here without my knowledge?'

Jubair rolls up his brown sleeves. Rashid trembles and looks around for signs of people who could stop Jubair from beating him up.

'Did you convince your sister? If not, how dare you shamelessly try to bury her here?'

'I tried, my brother. I tried. But you are already married. And she doesn't want to marry you.'

Jubair laughs and rubs his chin.

'Okay. No problem. But I cannot just let you go. I have to teach you a lesson.'

'Please, please, please don't beat me up!' Rashid prostrates before him and kisses the black shoes.

'I won't. Don't worry. Just throw the body into the river and we will be settled.'

'What? No, I can't!'

'Should I make your sister pay for damaging my land, then?'

Rashid's blue trousers now turn a shade darker. Jubair laughs with infrequent snorts in between.

'Listen, brother. Just because you are not right in the head doesn't mean I will let you go. Do it now or else I will not only beat you up but also make your lovely sister pay.'

'Please. Let me and my mother go. I will never come here.'

'I can't. I must teach you a lesson. Ahh I can't wait to hold that smooth hair of hers when I make her my wife!'

Rashid's vision is blurry. He pushes away the image of Jubair's hand around Rahima's hair. He blinks hard, and yet it doesn't leave his eyes. He drags his mother's body by the legs towards the river. Tears dot the white shroud. It looks like Sharmin's corpse has been crying. After he throws the corpse and droplets of the murky river perch on his face, his body trembles more than before, as if it were him under water.

Queen Victoria

She was sitting atop a grey wall with mossy splotches when Fatima and Faiz first saw her on their way home from school. She yawned and licked her furry face. Then she fixed her resolute green-eyed gaze on them as if scanning the contents of their thirteen-year-old souls. She couldn't be from here. A long, fluffy, healthy and foreign-looking cat in Mohammadpur? No. Perhaps one of the army officers posted here in Dacca bought it from a fancy pet shop in Karachi and it fled the house. Perhaps.

'I think its name should be Queen Victoria,' Fatima said as they solved math homework under a fiery haze in the study room Baba had assigned for them.

'True,' Faiz replied in a low clipped voice as was his usual manner of speaking.

When they saw her the second time, Fatima unzipped her Pink Panther bag and took out her tiffin box. She placed the half-eaten sandwich at the grassy base of the wall like an offering at a temple. The cinnamon-coloured cat looked downwards and leapt off the wall. It smelled and took apart the sandwich, eating only the generous bits of chicken inside. A sense of accomplishment crept up Fatima's legs and climbed into her soul.

'Should we take it home, Faiz?'

He stared at her, blankness splashed across his face.

'I think we should,' she added. And when she held the cat by its front arms and put it in her bag and no protest was issued from Faiz and the cat itself, she felt confident. That One, she wasn't stealing someone else's cat because the cat made itself comfortable inside the bag willingly. That Two, Faiz's approval meant he would support her in keeping Queen Victoria's presence hidden from Baba, who had told them time and again that they shouldn't bother asking him for things unless they score at least ninety per cent in their final examinations. As for Maryam, the twenty-year-old maid who had been taking care of them since they were five-years-old squeaky children, she wouldn't be an issue. Didn't she protect them and pray for them in the light of all the things they had to endure? Yes, she did. Despite being East Pakistani, she spoke Urdu well enough to get employed in the house. Sometimes, the twins thought she wasn't a Bangali but a pure Urdu-speaking Pakistani, one of their own.

Maryam shrieked as they slid out of their shoes and ran upstairs to Fatima's room with this cloud-like creature.

'What is it doing here?' she said, wide-eyed, hands on waist.

'Isn't she beautiful? Meet Queen Victoria!' Fatima replied. Faiz fetched water from the bathroom and placed the red bowl on the bed. Queen Victoria lapped it up like it had been without water for days.

'Your father! I bet he will ship you to where Queen Victoria is now. Grave!'

Maryam fumed and hurried out of the room with her plait violently cutting the air.

Fatima's shoulders drooped, the smile leached away from her face. Faiz, unbothered, caressed Queen Victoria's back.

In the evening, an hour before Baba came home from his glass factory, Maryam's heart melted – not for the cat but for the children – and she offered them an extra packet of Marie biscuits to dip into their tea as peace offering and a plan was hatched. Queen Victoria (who, as declared by Maryam by now, was a female and was not in need of a name change) was to stay with Maryam in her room downstairs.

They didn't sleep that night. Once Baba kissed them on the foreheads and said his 'I Love Yous' and locked his bedroom door with a full bottle of maroon brandy and his silver liquor flask, Fatima jumped out of her bed and signalled Faiz to come with her downstairs. They whisked raw chicken from the refrigerator, peeled two bananas, and watched Queen Victoria gorge herself on the food. The dim yellow light and Fatima's undying giggles annoyed Maryam.

'Tch, go to sleep or I'll scream,' Maryam said from time to time with a subdued voice, a pillow resting over her ears. All night long, they fed her in batches, brushed her with Maryam's combs (without Maryam's knowledge), kissed her, caressed her, watched her in astonishment, climbed Maryam's steel cupboard (an activity to which Queen Victoria and her audience seemed addicted), watched her jump back down, took her to the backyard and witnessed, with horror, her mauling to death three white mice, accidentally let her out of the room, losing her in the darkness of the dining room and living room and painstakingly salvaging her from under a bandy-legged sofa, and finally, relaxed with her on the white swing, a cool breeze brushing their bodies.

Dawn came over, bringing with it the cawing of crows and the azan rising out of the mosque two blocks away. Faiz started dozing off, his head leaning on Fatima's shoulder. Fatima pinched his bare thigh.

'Ow.'

'Let's go upstairs now. Or else Maryam will lecture us about praying Fajr.'

So, they placed Queen Victoria beside a snoring Maryam, who, unsurprisingly, couldn't wake up for Fajr on account of the nocturnal disturbance, shut the door and ran upstairs. They showered, arranged their bags and fell flat on their beds to catch a thirty-minute nap until the driver rang the bell and ferried their bleary-eyed selves to school in Baba's black Ambassador.

'Roll number 48!' the math teacher shouted, like he shouted every other roll number in the class.

'Take it,' he said, his jaws busily breaking milk candies, handing over the thin white exam script to Faiz.

An F plastered on the front page of his copy. He got six out of hundred in his math midterm exam.

Fatima knew what his result would be. The usual F. It was because of the mercy and warmth of Baba's fat notes that the school always allowed Faiz re-tests and generous marking in those re-tests and eventually, promotion. She didn't look at his copy once he sat beside her, his hands firmly placed on the cover page, his gaze lowered. She feared that looking at his copy might put some sort of curse on hers. When she received hers, she was relieved for a D. Thirty-three. But she was also unsettled. Like Faiz was. Like Maryam would be once they told her about the F and D.

They walked home under the blazing sun because the Ambassador was with Baba at his glass factory in Savar. A cloud of silence stalked them. Faiz crouched beside the drain bordering the paddy field and puked once twice thrice, disgorging his breakfast. Fatima patted his head as if that would be a great deal of help. They resumed their walk, leaving behind a trail of urine slithering down Faiz's navy-blue trousers. This was a routine chain of events every time (read: always) the Fs and Ds glared at the twins from their math copies.

Once they were home, Maryam didn't need to ask about the wetness of the trousers and gloominess of the faces.

She groaned and muttered curses under her breath while dipping their clothes in and out of a plastic bucket saturated with detergent.

'For the love of God, for ONCE can they NOT do terrible results? And their father... that man my god... why doesn't he die?'

When Baba was home and kissed them on their foreheads and said his 'I Love Yous' to which the twins also (although reluctantly and with a heavy weight of fear on their lips) replied 'I Love Yous', Maryam, still clad in her floral prayer gown, peeped from the kitchen and prayed to God so He may PLEASE save the children.

'The results came today, right?'

'Ji Baba,' Fatima replied, stunned at how he never missed the date.

'How did it go?'

Gazes lurking on the mosaic dots. Silence unspooling from their cores, spreading in every direction inside the bungalow.

He dropped his suitcase on the floor and bit his lips, which mostly remained hidden owing to his bushy moustache. He went into the study, his boots stomping the ground, and held the door open, waiting for the twins to follow. Before they entered, they looked at Maryam, who was now teary, her hand clasped over her mouth.

Inside, the twins leaned over the circular wooden desk with a silver flower vase at the centre. Fatima clenched her jaws and thought about Queen Victoria. How she must be munching on boiled carrots under Maryam's bed now. Faiz thought about his bladder. How it will loosen very soon, on account of the fear frothing inside him, and lo and behold, a stream of hot urine will befoul the floor, and Maryam will have to clean up his shame later.

The wooden ruler first landed on Faiz's buttocks. Then it landed on Fatima's thighs (yes, Baba was considerate enough to stop hitting her buttocks after she turned eleven and parts of her body started jutting out). Twenty calculated blows for Faiz and ten for Fatima.

From outside, Maryam heard the ruler meeting their bodies. It sounded as though a dirty mattress was being beaten with a stick. She winced and let out soft moans of agony, which increased with Fatima's wail. Unlike Fatima, Faiz always cried quietly.

Baba believed in the supremacy of grades over all things that made up one's childhood. Much like his father, he did not want his children to grow up academically challenged. He did not want his children to inherit his wealth and ruin it with their incompetence. Memories sped through his mind when he beat his children. The sixth grade. An F in mathematics and C in English. His father's leather whips on his arms and buttocks. The seventh grade. Below fifty per cent in the final examination. Whole winter vacation spent in the village with unknown relatives he had never met and latrines he had mistaken for chicken coops. The eighth grade. The fear of his father's wrath tangling around his heart. A ninety per cent in the final examination! He was convinced that fear was the best medicine.

School was off for an indefinite period of time because of the grievances of the East Pakistani people and their organized strikes to hold the West Pakistan authority accountable for illegally undermining the Eastern wing's autonomy, as the radio had announced on Sunday morning.

Which meant joy. Except for the fact that Baba had to stay home for the most part because his factory shut down once the strikes erupted.

Queen Victoria was now allowed outside (but never upstairs) only after 8 p.m., after Baba retired to his room with his increased alcohol intake.

The first time she had a brush with falling under Baba's eyes was when the power had gone out in the entire neighbourhood. Fatima was coaxing it to 'please just eat a little more!' She stalked her through the dimly lit hallway with a bowl of steamed rice arranged in tiny balls. And then the power went out. She disappeared, leaving in her wake an untraceable thread of meows. Fatima's stomach turned. She thought she would empty her insides in the hall. No, Baba cannot find her. The warm redness of her thighs from the wooden ruler blows had barely healed. With Faiz's gold-rimmed torchlight, they scanned the entire house. Even Baba's room. Thankfully, he did not enquire why they were snooping around because who would smoke a liberal amount of Marlboro on the balcony and speak with his girlfriend then? The power returned after three hours, and Queen Victoria was found choking and tossing two grey mice behind the almond tree.

The second time was Maryam's fault. Couldn't she have put the pressure cooker on after bathing the Queen? The wet furry nuisance sauntered about the house when it observed that damn, this dumb lady has forgot ten to shut the door properly. It gracefully made its way to Baba's room and lounged on the balcony in the afternoon sun. Baba saw it but didn't do anything. It's a hallucination, Akbar. The liquor splashing and swooshing and wobbling inside your head is making you see things. Like your dead wife. Whom you saw just yesterday! In her red lehenga and gold bangles! But you have to think about things that matter. Your wife doesn't matter anymore. She stopped mattering when she flew out of this world right after the twins came out of her. And just like that, how is a cat significant? You have to think about your factory! If these strikes continue, you can kiss your hard-earned wealth goodbye and (sorry to say, ahem) go live with your parents in Karachi and listen to your ex-judge/eternal-landlord father taunt you about leeching off his wealth like a parasite!

The third time, well, it wasn't a brush as much as it was a full-blown discovery. His girlfriend, a woman with a strong Lahori accent, had come over. He was buttering her up for the past few weeks because her father, top-brass in the Pakistan army, could sure make some arrangements for her boyfriend, couldn't he? Maryam and the twins did not know what went on inside the bedroom. Gross. They didn't need to know.

It felt like an un-worded shock, a betrayal. To see their father with another woman who was not their Ammu. In Maryam's room, the twins were subdued. Faiz glassily stared at his tattered copy of *Charlie and the Chocolate Factory*, without turning a single page. Fatima sat on the porch outside the room and twisted the ribbon of her frock around her index finger. Queen Victoria chewed and fumbled with the rubber ball as if it were a dead sparrow.

Fatima got up and went into the kitchen, leaving Faiz in charge of Queen Victoria.

'Maryam. Will Baba bring us a new Ammu?'

She pretended to ignore her question and stirred the onions sizzling in the oil.

She tugged her *orna*.

'Answer me. Will he marry that woman?'

'Ahhaa. Why do you think so much, huh? Who told you to think such thoughts?'

'I don't like that woman.'

'Guess what? Me neither.'

'I don't like how her eyebrows look like snakes.'

'Did you notice her hair? It looks like a damn haystack!'

They giggled, hands on each other's shoulders. Then the woman's shrill screams wafted from upstairs.

They saw her crouching by the railing, her screams still persistent. Queen Victoria, as bold as she was, kept meowing in front of her. Faiz hurried up the stairs. Fatima pinched his arm and slapped his head. 'What on earth were you doing?' He trembled, rubbing the edges of his Roald Dahl book. 'You were still reading after I left?' she pulled at his collars. Baba emerged out of the room and disconnected the call he was attending to. 'What happened?' he said, his face wrinkled with concern, and moved towards his girlfriend, wrapped her in his arms.

'This stupid cat! What is it doing here? Please get this thing out of my sight!' she said, wetness and makeup mingled on her face. 'What are you looking at?' he asked Maryam. 'How the hell did it get inside? Are you a duffer?'

'Brother, I don't know. It must have come through the backyard,' she replied.

Queen Victoria kept meowing like she was enjoying the spectacle that arose from her presence. Baba retrieved his arms from his girlfriend, picked up Queen Victoria by her pink collar (which Maryam had made from Fatima's old frocks' ribbons), headed with a wincing and still-meowing Queen Victoria towards the veranda beside Faiz's room, and threw her, like a frisbee, into the hot afternoon. She swirled over the small backyard and landed with her belly on the pikes atop the white compound walls. Maryam later mopped the blood staining the wall over which Queen Victoria had fallen and prayed to God to send the man to hell for this killing.

Maryam took a week off. Her father was sick. Most probably dengue. Her mother suspected he would kick the bucket soon. Fatima's days were spent praying her five daily prayers, supplicating, and speaking to God (through which she mostly beseeched Him to reunite her with Queen Victoria in heaven). After Queen Victoria's death, life became a meaningless burden she hadn't signed up for. She learned all the Islamic rituals and rules from Maryam of her own volition. It pleasantly surprised Maryam that all these years of pushing these twins to start practising their religion finally started paying off, partly. Maryam gave Fatima her copy of the Qur'an with both Bangla and Urdu translations inside. She fashioned a prayer gown for her with the sewing machine on the back porch using an old bedsheet. She showed her how to rinse the mouth, wash the nostrils, hands, face, feet and wipe the head and ears with wet fingers during wudu. She taught her how to perform the mandatory ritual bath after every nocturnal emission and period spell.

There was no sign of spiritual awakening in Faiz. He retreated into himself even more. He spoke only with 'Yes' and 'No'. He biked throughout the neighbourhood. He stopped saying 'I Love Yous' to Baba (to which Baba hadn't expressed any objection). He imagined scenarios where Baba died. Slipping on the rooftop on a rainy day and falling on the car. Getting a heart attack while smoking. Getting bitten by a snake or hit by a truck or hacked to death by robbers on his morning walk.

In the afternoons, Fatima and Faiz unrolled a pink mat on the grass and lounged with *Alice's Adventures*, *The Little Prince*,

Charlotte's Web, *Anne of Green Gables*, *The Jungle Book* and some Roald Dahl scattered between them. Their eyes walked over the letters. Their minds roamed elsewhere. They preferred Maryam's presence. Although it wouldn't quell the pain of not having Queen Victoria around, it would at least allow them to forget her death for a brief period. Before Queen Victoria came to their lives, they spent the afternoons acting out *The Jungle Book* with Maryam in the yard looping around the bungalow. Maryam would be Sher Khan, chasing Faiz (Baloo) and Fatima (Mowgli) for a while. Then Fatima and Faiz would rise to the occasion and launch themselves against Maryam. Sometimes Maryam took them to the banks of the river where they would race, watch roving circus shows that involved monkeys fighting one another and snakes (occasionally), eat roasted peanuts, fly kites and ride on horses for free because the horse keeper was Maryam's cousin. Now the absence of Maryam and Queen Victoria was a hand on their necks. It pinched and reminded them of the long stretches of time they would have to paddle.

Four days after Maryam left, Faiz woke up in the middle of the night, droplets of sweat crowding his forehead. He had seen a nightmare in which Baba was beating Queen Victoria on the driveway with his golf club. Queen Victoria shouted, 'Help me, Faiz! Please! Won't you?' 'Hey, shut up!' Baba said and continued beating, blood gathering at his feet like floodwater.

Faiz washed his face, in a vain attempt to forget the nightmare. He took a pair of scissors from his desk. He skittered into Baba's room, which was, thankfully, unlocked tonight. Half of Baba's body dangled from the sofa chair. His silver liquor flask and an empty bottle of brandy lay on the carpet. Flies hovered over the biscuits, nuts and empty glass on the coffee table. Faiz opened his cupboard. Took out his olive suit. Ripped a hole in the middle. Left the violated piece on the bed.

Faiz understood the gravity of his action only after it was done. Now he was thinking Ish! What a fool! You should have thought this through! Now where will you go? What will you do when Baba the Monster starts torturing you? Pretty sure your buttocks will explode this time. What if he brings out his bamboo cane? Or that whip he keeps hidden somewhere in the study? And no, don't even think about peeing in this room. I know your bladder is twisting and turning. But no. Have some shame. Can't commit crimes consecutively.

Faiz relieved himself in the washroom, thinking if he should really bike his way to Maryam's at this hour. He can hear foxes howling on the street from the open window above the commode. Did he even remember the slum by the rail station where Maryam's family lived? He and Fatima went there last year, despite Maryam's insistence that no, they shouldn't leave without Baba's permission. Think, Faiz, think. Oh wait, there it is. The second alley from the front gate of the station, wasn't it? The tin house with the coppery gate and tin roof with wild creepers? You must go.

In the backyard, Fatima, sat on the swing, pondered over Faiz's note, which said, 'I cut Baba's suit. Shouldn't have. Now leaving for Maryam's. Don't tell Baba where I am.' When and how did her brother turn out to be this bold?

Squirrels chirped in the almond trees overhead. Robins and parakeets stitched the clear morning sky. She thought of Queen Victoria. How, if she were alive, none of this would have happened. The suit cutting. The fugitiveness of Faiz. How they could all simply enjoy this day in the backyard. Tears gathered behind her eyes. She raised her hands.

And trembled. She asked God to miraculously diminish Baba's rage so she could go fetch Faiz, telling him it was okay to return. Faiz, he won't beat you up.

Many times, throughout the day she thought Baba had died. So, she went into his room often and put her finger under his nostrils. Still breathing. Puffy eyes. Thin clean-shaven cheeks. Lines on the forehead. Wavy eyebrows. So innocent. Remnants of his juvenile self on the face minus the bushy moustache. Who could think this face was capable of so much violence? Fatima decided it was best to throw away the suit. He could not blame her, Faiz and Maryam for the missing suit without compelling evidence. Well, he could, actually, and terrorize the three in the process or even fire Maryam for thievery, but the most urgent matter was to save Faiz's backside from Baba's torture tools. She wanted to bring Faiz back while the daylight was still out. But she feared that if Baba woke up suddenly and found the house empty, he would call his connections in the army and have them turn Dacca upside down to search for his children.

Baba woke up at 10 p.m. He kissed Fatima on the forehead and said I Love You. She replied the same. 'Where is Faiz?' he asked before going back into his room.

'He's on the rooftop,' Fatima lied. She bit the insides of her cheeks. Would he go check now?

Baba went to the living room downstairs. She let out a long breath and said a stream of 'Alhamdulillah, Praise be to God'.

An hour later, Baba hurried upstairs. Fatima had just finished praying Isha. Hands raised, she was in the middle of supplicating when Baba entered the room.

'Fatima, bolt all the windows, quick!' he said.

'But what happened, Baba?' she asked, rising from her prayer mat.

'There's a war of sorts. The military is on the streets,' he replied, tense, fumbling with the radio antennae to get better signal on the news.

Fatima's mind was blank. Her hands and legs shivered as she bolted shut all the windows. Was Faiz safe? Maryam? Should she tell Baba that Faiz had left the house? But be careful, Fatima. You can't tell him you lied. Just tell him you discovered the note just now. Maybe he can use his contacts to retrieve Faiz and Maryam – and her family – from the chaos outside.

A faint din of gunfire floating in. It grew heavy as time passed by. The grumble of military tanks and trunks saturated the cool air. Flashes of orange blared on the horizon. Dark pillars of smoke climbed the distant night sky. Fatima closed the veranda door and ran into Faiz's room. She tore a page from his English copy and wrote, in cursive to imitate Faiz's handwriting, 'Leaving for Maryam's. Will be back soon.' With all the fear raging in her cells, the handwriting lacked perfect resemblance to Faiz's.

She approached Baba in the living room. He was huddled over the radio, still jerking the antennae for better signal. 'Baba, look. Faiz... he wrote this. He had told me he was on the rooftop. But... I saw it just now,' she said, breaking down. Her chest heaved as she sobbed. As though she had just gotten a good amount of beating from Baba for getting a D in math.

Baba's face wrinkled. But why under God would Faiz leave without his permission? You must investigate it later. You can beat him up all you want then. But first, for the love of God, find your son. Call your contacts and get him out of that stinky railway ghetto!

Fatima's sob trickled to a whimper. The world around her was a blur. First, Queen Victoria, and now, the possibility of losing Faiz (and Maryam). From whatever scraps she could gather, Baba had called one Mr Aziz, one Mr Sheherzade, one Mr Rabbani, among many other important-sounding men in the army.

'But my son... you must understand. I have to find him.'

'He can't be out there! You have to do something!'

'My son isn't even a Bangali! You folks are killing THEM, not a pure Pakistani like him, goddamnit!'

'These imbeciles! How can they not help their own people? Ball-less devils!' Baba shouted to himself, pulling at the roots of his greying hair.

Baba took the car keys from the nail under the taxidermy deer. He lit a cigarette to calm himself. Fatima accompanied him as he hopped inside the Ambassador and drove out of the neighbourhood. He didn't reprimand her for risking her life.

Outside, cars were burning. Jeeps, trucks, and tanks lined the roads. Piles of dead bodies – some burning, some not burning – cropped up here and there like mounds of hay. Baba had to steer through the haze of smoke on several streets. Gunfire sounds cupped the car. The immediacy of it all made Fatima want to disappear into the leather seat. Maryam's house wasn't far away. But the chaos made the distance seem tremendous.

A blockade of trucks and tanks near the railway station. Baba parked the car in front of the soldiers keeping guard. He flashed his passport and said, 'My son is inside. Don't stop me.'

'I'm sorry, sir. I can't let you in,' one soldier replied.

'How dare you? First your hypocrite officers don't help me get my son out of this massacre and now you tell me I can't do it myself. Get out of my way.'

'Sir. We have to follow a protocol. You have to understand.'

'To hell with your protocol,' he shouted. At this point, tears left his eyes, soaking his pink face.

Fatima, in the meantime, sprinted through a gap between the soldiers, who aimed their guns at her.

'Hey! Don't shoot! That's my daughter, you morons,' he screamed, his voice now raspy.

She ran towards Maryam's house, smoke filling her lungs, the warmth of burning fires lashing at her skin.

Baba and three soldiers followed.

The road leading to her house was bloated with corpses. She tripped on four of them. She looked like the dead, with all the blood on her hands, face and the prayer gown she hadn't changed out of.

When she reached the slum, her house wasn't identifiable. The slum was an ocean of fire, sizzling and snapping wood, bamboo, tin, bones. She coughed. She tried to go inside. The black smoke bellowing sporadically out of the fire repelled her.

Fatima sat on the ground. Fingered the dust beneath her palms. A dead girl lay beside her in a pool of blood. Her mouth open, blood still dripping from her face. Just like Queen Victoria.

Behind, Baba lost himself.

'No, no, no, no, no! This can't be happening. No! Faiz! Where are you? My son, please come out! I won't beat you for leaving without permission! I promise! I won't beat you ever again! Please come out, son! I love you!'

He attempted to go inside. The soldiers held him down. In the fiery glow, his face glistened. As though it were melting in grief.

Panda

The girl doesn't hug her father – her only parent – before hurrying to school today. Let him sleep, she thinks. She further thinks: Poor man guarded his sugarcane orchard all night with a kerosene lamp and a bamboo stick against any potential elephant attacks. Could I do that to ensure food for my children's bellies? Never!

She ties her shoelaces and exhales upon opening the door. The rains have turned the roads into a lake of coffee. She can't miss school. She has her final English exam. So, she hitches up her white skirt and runs out of the hut. The water paints her uniform brown anyway.

Wading tightens the muscles of her legs. She decides to climb up the slope beside the road and run through the forest at the base of the hills. The brick building is visible. Inside, students are shrinking their umbrellas and those without umbrellas are shivering. The exam hasn't started yet. She relaxes her walk now. She parts the taro and bamboo leaves in front of her legs and eyes. A rustle in the back. Is a leopard upon her? No. They were last seen a decade ago. She turns. It's a man in a black raincoat. He presses her face with a white handkerchief that smells tangy and sweet.

*

At Jenkins & Milburn Academy, Kaniz is the only girl without a Panda. And therefore, friends. She is in the ninth grade, and she wishes she had a Panda so she could invite the whole class to her apartment behind the water tanks – okay, no, scratch that. Did Giovanni live in an apartment? Lilly? Morrison? Abigail? Did Erin? Did Jack? Michael? Every soul in the class lived inside gated colonies scattered throughout West Sacramento. They lived in houses with spires and granite chimneys. Their parents owned corporations that drilled oil, mined copper and cut timber in Asia and Africa. She couldn't bring upon her a new variant of humiliation at the cost of showing off a Panda.

Her grades have been suffering since time immemorial, but Kona, her mother, has never raised her voice. She only said, 'Do better next time, my girl!' Gabriel, her father, was too social with the outside world to care about his family. He was hardly home. His routine involved: going to the office early in the morning, leaving at night, getting sloshed at bars with friends and listening to Kona's tearful rebukes in the morning before leaving for office and repeating the cycle. Apparently, he was so social that one day he left home and sent a text to Kona that he was going to Asia with his friends to find himself and she should totally start seeing other guys and no, she shouldn't worry about his finances because he was *carpe diem*-ing his adventures with the savings from his job.

With her grades, today is no exception. Kaniz is seated on the couch, her gaze lost, her popcorn turning soft and rubbery on the coffee table, the TV blaring a reality show where people put makeup on their Pandas and judges eliminate those whose Pandas end up looking like glittery Christmas cushions. 'Do better next time, my girl!' Kona says, ruffling Kaniz's red hair, which, by the way, looks ghastly on her,

Kona thinks. She prefers her half-Bangladeshi black hair to this abomination. But she cannot say anything about it because she thinks perhaps it's her way of coping with the recent departure of her father. However, Kaniz would not experience a slight flutter in her soul even if her father was discovered having secret affairs with multiple women simultaneously. She was sure he had forgotten her birthday and how she looked. His presence was like a benevolent shadow's. A shadow that supplied them with additional money on top of Kona's income as a junior accountant at a local bank. Besides this specific generosity, Kona craved for Gabriel to be an active – a proper – husband and father.

Kaniz doesn't tell Kona that she is not upset about her final report card. It is Imogen's birthday next week. The whole class is invited except her. Later that week, they are flying to British Columbia for the annual and unofficial Jenkins & Milburn Academy Panda Convention where they will dance to EDM under the northern lights, roast marshmallows, hike up the hills with their Pandas, buy earrings, wigs, sunglasses, jackets and skateboards for their Pandas, etc., etc., etc. She wants to repeat to Kona (like she has told her for the past couple of years) how she has been missing out on such joys ever since she was enrolled at the private school in the fifth grade and how she has had enough and how she wants to enjoy like them from now on because life ought to give her a chance. She doesn't say anything.

She bounds towards her room and sobs into her pillow. She knows ranting about her desire to fully integrate into the private school will be fruitless. It was hard enough for Kona to send her daughter to a private school (even with Gabriel's income). Interests and the prospects of new loans for rent stalked Kona. Kaniz could not suddenly expect her mother to show up with a Panda and keys to a mansion so she would not have to eat lunch alone at school beside the cafeteria entrance.

Her sobs weaken. She slides into an unplanned afternoon nap. And dreams of a world where she is inviting the whole class to her birthday party in the sloping, grassy backyard where they can slip out of their clothing and jump into the infinity pool (with inflated pink swans and floating trays of cocktails) overlooking oaks and pines and sycamores and tiny cars bounding up the zigzagging roads. They will exhaust their necks from counting the windows of her house. They will get lost within the corridors full of rooms and bathrooms. They will want to touch her gold-necklaced Panda and make a line to carry it in turns. They will invite her to their birthday parties, the next Convention, sit with her in class, at the cafeteria.

Her face is sticky when she wakes up. The flowery curtains, the croaking single bed, and the weathered white cupboard scream her unbelongingness at the school. She slides open her phone to numb her pain with baby videos and memes. When she is bombarded with ads about the Pandas, she turns it off.

She eyes through the glass a Panda on display from outside the store. She wants to touch the stuffed animal without the tall white-haired man looking and eventually dragging her out like he did (while pinching her arms) three years ago. She especially wants to touch what makes these stuffed animals so special: their eyes. Blue eyes. Yellow eyes. Brown. Emerald. Silver. Purple.

When they first came out, all every news channel could talk about was these stuffed animals' eyes and the exorbitant prices. The company – P & McIntosh Associates – quickly rose to popularity as celebrities and rich people flocked to buy these animals whose eyes seemed real like it were a living being. While an economy revolving around the production of these stuffed animals began flourishing globally, environmental and human rights activists called for a complete ban on the company for its probable ties to organ harvesting from humans and other species.

'I want to assure you all that none of these allegations are true. These eyes look real because of the wonderful work our sister company, P Visuals Ltd, does,' the CEO said at a press conference in the company's meeting room in the Empire State Building.

His blonde hair turned orange on occasions when protestors threw canned soup and ketchup. The company's lawyers showed the journalists present inside the courtroom a list of movies whose gory and graphic costumes P Visuals Ltd created and how realistic the zombies, sea monsters and human gorillas looked. With time, the protests subsided because it was legally established that the company had not violated human and non-human rights.

The man's gaze locks with Kaniz's. Flints of embarrassment bloom inside her cheeks. She hurries out of view. A taxi hits her as she steps off the curb. She rolls over its windshield, travels all the way back.

At the hospital, she wakes up to a weeping Kona who is being comforted by Tully, her colleague from work. Kona is on her knees beside the bed when Kaniz wakes up. She rubs her hands and strokes her hair. She kisses the bridge of her nose, just below the bandage wrapping her forehead.

'Oh, my sweetheart.' She blows her nose into a tissue. 'How do you feel now? Do you want ice cream?'

'No, mom. I am completely fine.'

Kona locks her in a hug. 'I am so sorry this happened to you, love. I am so sorry.' Her tears drench a patch of Kaniz's hair.

The accident imprints on Kona's face a cold slap. Mortality is real, it says. You could die anytime. So could your daughter. One minute you are walking down the footpath, another minute you are crushed beneath a truck because the driver was too generous with his vodka consumption. So, why not live when you are alive? Hurry! Call P & McIntosh Associates! Didn't you see their advertisement the other day while logging out at the end of your shift at the bank? Didn't the perks include a free Panda that otherwise costs 1.5 million dollars? 1,30,000 dollars per annum as a senior accountant in their West Sacramento office? Are you worried about ethics? Oh c'mon! Firstly, there is no evidence that the company is involved with organ farming. Secondly, even if the farming bit is true, just because your childhood cat froze to death inside the sadistic neighbour's refrigerator, and you became acutely aware of the suffering of people and animals after the incident doesn't mean you should deprive your daughter of joys she craves. Be smart.

Two months later, Kona hands an architecture magazine to Kaniz and breaks the news that she has cleared the three rounds of written tests and two rounds of interviews and been hired by P. She asks Kaniz to pick the house she loves.

'Is it real, Mom? Will we be living in one of these houses?' Kaniz grabs Kona's hands and pulls them on her lap. Electric threads roil inside her heart.

'Yes, sweetheart! Our times of misery are over.' She kisses Kaniz's forehead.

Days before her birthday, she places invitation cards embossed with pines on every desk in the class. The students shuffle in their seats and murmur when they see the address. Jenna is the first one to say yes. Then Giovanni. Then others follow.

Their new house is a two-storey granite bungalow with five bedrooms and six bathrooms in total. When the afternoon sun beats down on it, it appears more royal than it usually looks. The swimming pool in the backyard, like Kaniz dreamed once, is rippling under the influence of inflatable swans and floating trays of cocktail. Beside the pool, an inflatable castle, trampoline and slide. Long tables boast roast shrimps, drumsticks and sushi. Two chocolate fountains with marshmallow and cotton candy stalls stand near the hedge separating this compound from the next, which belongs to an NBA star. Electronic music swooshes and swirls through the property until everyone's battery runs out and they lounge on the even, warm grass and the outdoor sofas and bean bags with drinks.

Kaniz has dressed her Panda in a blue muslin skirt and a crown with a gleaming diamond in the centre. Its blue eyes heighten the costume's lustre. Her classmates flash their cameras as Kaniz poses with the stuffed animal, interchanging between a simple smile with V fingers and a pout on the Panda's cheek.

This month, she gets invited to Lara, Ron and Kim's birthday parties following her official induction one lunchtime into the Panda Club, which ensures her access to the annual Panda Conventions. Rick, the aspiring basketball player, conducted her induction by calling her in front of the cafeteria and telling everyone to clap for their newest member whose 'Panda is, undoubtedly, the best dressed among everyone else's'. He starts dating Kaniz. He does not have a license, but he drives his father's Range Rover and takes her camping up on the hills late at night. Kaniz hides this from Kona and tells her that she's going out to one or another friend's place, which is also true because she now gets regular invites for stayovers.

She dyes her hair brown because Rick says that colour makes her look like a supermodel. The compliment inspires her to secretly throw Kona's lasagnes and pasta dishes into the bin for the raccoons and to tan herself with her girlfriends – either at the beach or pool sides – for social media. Her grades go up, which prompts Kona to say something along the lines of: 'Remember how I always said you'd do better next time? It's happening, girl!' On the weekends, Kaniz bakes chocolate ganache cakes for Kona as a token of appreciation for setting up in her life a beacon of happiness.

Kaniz has just received an Elton John special jacket for her stuffed Panda. She tears the package open with her mouth while walking up the corridor. Kona hasn't closed her bedroom door. Kaniz sees her crying. Kona pauses, looks at the ceiling, pushes aside tears and places her hand on her chest. Then she cries some more. Kaniz believes Kona is missing Gabriel. She doesn't know Kona is actually grieving over her job at P. Flashbacks of Babu, her childhood cat, batter Kona's head as she contemplates her job and her role in the violence.

Pam and David, her closest colleagues at the office, gave her insider information regarding the eyes' origins in the stuffed Pandas. Pam works at the Analytics Department while David is in charge of Human Resources for Asia. As such, they had to sign legally binding confidentiality forms whereby they declared their lips shall remain shut regarding P's operations. They told Kona because the trio knew each other through geography class back in high school and they were quitting the 'morally dark' job and they wanted her (not forcibly) to quit as well. 'Why do you think they pay the employees so generously? To seal their mouths!' Pam said after disclosing P's darkness. 'So, they don't quit the job upon discovering the unethical practices by chance. They will fatten you with money, Kona. And the money will make you blind.' Kona bashed a stapler on her desk. 'Do whatever the heck you want, girl. Quit! I don't care. I ain't leaving this job. I am happy. My daughter's happy.'

Pam locked her arms across her chest. 'You are already blind, sis.'

'I don't need your lecture, girl. You don't know the struggles of an immigrant family. My father dragged his bum all the way here from Bangladesh so we could live a better life. Now that we are living it, stop bothering me! Also, you two were here before me. You have been here longer than me. Stop acting so high and mighty now.' Kona grabbed a black file and left the room.

Why is mom not over that worthless man, she tells Rick that night over the phone. Maybe she needs another man in her life, Rick replies. The next day she fills out her details on the LoveNLaugh app for a date with one Oliver who is a corporate lawyer by day and novelist by night and looks like Adam Driver's long-lost twin. She does so because she thinks it is her responsibility to bring happiness to Kona's life because didn't mom make sure Kaniz got all the happiness she deserved? The date ends with Kona staying over at Oliver's place. Kaniz considers it a new, radiant beginning in her mother's life.

Kona brings Oliver to her place after the second date.

'Hello, Kaniz,' he says, stretching out his hand.

'Hi, Oliver. Thank you for making my mother happy.' She stretches hers and is awash with the coolness a parent feels in their heart when their child has finally found a friend at a new school.

She remains seated beside Oliver on the black sofa in front of the fireplace. Kaniz passes by the living room with the Panda in her arms because she will take its photo near the pool for a paid advertisement of the Panda's knotty lavender ribbons on social media. Oliver's eyes twitch. He scratches the sides of his index finger.

A slant of sunshine falling from the skylight warms the patch beside Kona. She rubs her eyes and calls Oliver. He is not in the washroom. She scratches her head, yawns. She finds the electric kettle empty, which is usually filled every morning by Kaniz.

'Hi, girl. Morning.'

'Morning, Mom.' Kaniz shuffles the flower vases, bow-legged chairs and side tables.

'What are you looking for, love?'

'I can't find my Panda, Mom. I can't.' A torrent of electricity buzzes in her nose. She purses her lips.

'Wait, I'll help you find it.' Kona walks out of the kitchen and joins Kaniz before ringing Oliver and finding his number out of network.

His face appears on news channels alongside three other men in the breaking news segments. They turn out to be a part of an underground organization called Warrior. Its aim is to 'liberate humans and non-humans from the exploitative practices of corporations and the rich'.

'Warrior has published a detailed document highlighting an unspeakable and unethical practice by P & McIntosh Associates. They have been farming human eyes from African and Asian villages, most recently from a cluster of villages near Borneo,' the anchor reads while stroking his navy blue tie.

'At nearly 300 pages, the document showcases the atrocities that P's men have inflicted upon the victims. It includes testimonials from the blind victims, ex-employees and former assaulters who were nabbed by the local police and intelligence forces collaborating with Warrior's intelligence department. The document contains graphic pictures that show how the victims' eyes were gouged after abduction and later processed and sterilized in factories with chemicals and colourful pigments.' The anchor exhales a long breath. 'Ms Wilkerson, this is quite the news. How reliable do you think this document is?'

'Well, as of now, we can safely assume the findings are legitimate. They have been at it for over five years, quietly at work to expose the company's practice. It sure serves as yet another reminder that the world cannot keep being the rich people's playground.' She swivels to the camera. 'Mr Hansen is reporting live from P & McIntosh Associates' New York office. Mr Hansen, could you please brief us about the situation there?'

'Mom, mom. Look, it's my Panda!' Kaniz hands her the phone. Her skin has turned pink. Kona wants to keep watching the news. She finds it unreal. Oliver's face on the TV screen, in particular. Something bitter cleaves her insides. She reluctantly turns her face away and zooms into the photo on Kaniz's phone. A warehouse full of beheaded and burnt Pandas shared from Warrior's social media page, now viral across newsfeeds. At the corner, quite visibly, lies Kaniz's Panda. It is wearing its crown with the gleaming diamond and the knotty lavender ribbons. The camera's flash is caught in the diamond's edge.

Kaniz wants to call Rick. She wants him to tell her that everything will be all right. Her hands sweat and tremble. She throws the phone on the sofa and buries her face in Kona's hair.

'It will be all right, love. Everything will be fine.' Kona brushes her hair.

Nothing will be all right, she wants to say. She will be kicked out of the Club. She will go back to being the lonely kid in the cafeteria. No Panda Convention for her. No birthday parties. No boyfriend.

Acknowledgements

I never thought I would end up writing a book, but here we are. All thanks to Almighty Allah, who made all of this possible, who brought into my life the following people:

My closest friends and readers without whose essential feedback and encouragement the stories perhaps wouldn't come to fruition: Shounak Reza, Tahsin Authoi, Maisha Nazifa Kamal, Tahsinul Islam Aurko, Neyamul Karim Tanveer, Sumaia Binte Islam, Ikhtisad Ahmed, Tanvi Srivastava, Meghna Nayar, Ulka Karandikar and Eshna Sharma. My wonderful editors who have given me supportive platforms for writing: Sarah Anjum Bari, Rifat Munim, Sohana Manzoor, Maya Palit, Roman Gautam, Minh Bui Jones, Scott Jordan and Marlon Ariyasinghe. My incredibly understanding agent: Kanishka Gupta and the Writer's Side team. My publishing editors Ashutosh Sharma, Anupama Manral and the entire Hachette India team for giving my debut a stellar home. My mentor Karan Mahajan for his comforting encouragement and constructive criticism that all writers require. Sonia Faleiro and the South Asia Speaks fellowship program for their immense generosity towards South Asian aspiring authors like myself. Aiysha Jahan, Nazneen Ahmed Pathak and Susmita Bhattacharya for giving me a fantastic community of writers and friends through the Write Beyond Borders program. Azmin Azran, Rumman R Kalam, Shahrukh Ikhtear and the entire *Shout* magazine team that gave me the chance to envision myself as a writer in the first place. My parents whose unconditional support in every step of the way made me question what I have ever done to deserve such a loving pair of parents. My country Bangladesh which, with its beauty and chaos and everything in between, provided me with a wealth of literary motivation. Lastly, the freedom fighters and the innocent civilians who died for the sake of liberating this country in 1971.